I0640525

TYLER ROBBINS

Evernight Publishing

www.evernightpublishing.com

Copyright© 2012 Tyler Robbins

ISBN: 978-1-77130-103-9

Cover Artist: Sour Cherry Designs

Editor: Karyn White

TYLER ROBBINS

DEDICATION

I would sincerely like to thank a special couple, Jeff and Charlene W.

When you came to me with this subject matter in mind, my first instincts were to run for the hills. But the seed had been planted and once my muse locked onto to Jared and Michael… well the story was inevitable.

Jeff, I can't thank you enough for your dedicated service to our country.

Charlene, what can I say, honey? You totally rock! I thank you for your support and for being a loyal cheerleader.

I would also like to thank my *"sister from another mister"*, Avril Ashton. Your eagle-eye and sharp wit have seen me through some dark and dreary manuscripts and this one especially benefitted from your no-nonsense critiquing skills. You are amazing, my friend!

TYLER ROBBINS

BEYOND HONOR

Tyler Robbins

Copyright © 2012

Chapter One

Army Medic, Private Michael Crest stretched his legs out across the sofa as he glared at the television, leaving little room for anyone to join him should they enter the barrack's common area. Any other night, traffic through the building would be a lot heavier if not for the bad weather preceding the expected landfall of Tropical Storm Constance. Half the state was on alert, including the Texas base he temporarily called home.

The lights flickered off and on as the wind kicked up outside. Horizontal lines wiggled across the screen of the ancient television, causing the news anchor to blur in and out of focus.

Michael considered heading home to his shared living quarters in the barracks, but his roommate, Joel Stratton, had company. Stratton's girlfriend, Alana, would only stay until curfew at twenty-three hundred hours anyway, and Michael had no intentions of spoiling their date. They hadn't spent a lot of time together since Alana had started her new position at the bank, so Michael didn't mind giving them space.

A loud clap of thunder rattled the windows. If

predictions were correct, Tropical Storm Constance, positioned a couple hundred miles off the coast of Texas, would make landfall by the end of the week. Michael would officially be on block leave well before then, and his plans to head north looked better and better by the minute.

Without warning, the door to the outside entrance of the day room swung open and slammed against the wall from the force of the unrelenting wind.

He sprang to his feet. His heart, already pumping double-time, skipped a beat when Specialist Jared Prophet crossed the threshold.

Of all the guys to interrupt his temporary escape from the daily grind, it had to be the one guy Michael hated to be alone with. Not because Jared made for bad company, but because Michael's attraction to the six-foot two-inch soldier had a tendency to send blood rushing to his groin, leaving his cock twitching with need.

Need that would go unfulfilled.

Jared Prophet, unapproachable on his best day, dripped with rugged, masculine bravado. Qualities Michael unfortunately found himself easily drawn to. The sex-god's sharp jawbone accentuated his chiseled, gladiator-like features.

Conjuring images of Jared Prophet in a leather loincloth did little to ease the instant heaviness of desire that sank below his belt and settled in his balls.

"Gettin' bad out there, huh?" Michael spoke first.

Jared's hollow glare punched Michael right in the gut.

Jared shut the door and silently stalked over to the Coke machine across from where Michael stood, unsure if he should say something else or shut the hell up and sit back down on the sofa.

"I don't think it'll get as bad as they say. The

weather's been too cool." Okay, he would ramble on like the idiot only Jared Prophet forced him to become.

Jared deposited coins into the machine and waited for his soda to drop to the bottom.

Michael cleared his throat. His heart boomed, and his stomach churned as though the storm outside had suddenly invaded his body.

Jared popped open the top of the can of Coke, guzzled it down, and tossed the empty can in the trash bin. His gaze then zeroed in on Michael. "Got any smokes?"

The man's gravelly timbre vibrated against Michael's tightened balls. Simply hearing him speak did things to Michael's body no other guy's voice ever had.

He slid two fingers into his shirt pocket and pulled out a pack of Marlboro Reds. "Yeah."

Jared cocked half a grin, and crescent moon creases ricocheted across his right cheek. "Can I bum one off of ya', dude?"

You can have whatever the hell you want. "Sure, man, no problem." Michael stepped forward and met Jared halfway across the room. "Here, there's only a couple left. You can have 'em."

Jared's brow arched as though intrigued by the gesture. "Nah, man I don't wanna take your last two smokes."

Michael's heart pumped wildly. He held his breath to settle the excitement and handed the cigarettes to Jared. "I have another pack. It's no big deal." He dug in his other pocket and held up a new, unopened box.

Jared took the other one, slid them into his back pocket and gave a firm nod to Michael. "Thanks, man."

Michael nodded back, too scared shitless to speak, afraid he'd say something stupid again.

"No sense in ruining a perfectly good cigarette

tryin' to smoke it out in that shit," Jared grumbled. "C'mon, Private, let's go back to high school."

Michael cocked his head to the side. "High school?"

Jared gestured for Michael to follow, which he was more than happy to do, like a loyal puppy trotting after his master.

He followed Jared into the men's bathroom.

Jared headed across the room and disappeared into the last stall on the right. In seconds, he rose above the cubicle, standing on the toilet as he raised the window above it. "Well, don't just stand there, kid, unless you want to set off the smoke alarm."

Panic zapped across Michael's skin. Was he really about to enter a bathroom stall with Jared Prophet, the sexiest guy on base? *Fuck yeah.* He might be a lot of things, but stupid wasn't one of them.

"With the weather so bad, none of those dumb fucks are gonna come in here tonight." Jared hopped down from the toilet and leaned against the side wall. He reached into his pocket and pulled out a silver Zippo lighter.

A white stream of smoke drifted upward from Jared's parted lips and danced into his nostrils as he inhaled.

Michael swallowed hard and lit his own cigarette, but not with nearly the James Dean flair Jared had mastered.

Smoke drifted toward the widow and was sucked out by whirls of hot, stormy air. "You're right. Not many people will be out in this weather."

Jared shook his head and smiled. "Not anyone with sense anyway. Guess that's why *we're* here."

"I couldn't sleep." Michael drew in another deep drag.

"There's no place like home, huh, kid?"

Michael eyed him closely. For the second time, Jared had called him "kid". "Nah, it ain't that." He squared his five feet ten inch stance. Jared still towered over him. No wonder he looked at him as though he were still a kid. "I get these feelings sometimes, like—" Michael stopped. *What am I doing?* Had he almost told the object of his lust he had a sickening feeling in his gut that something bad was about to happen? *He'll think I'm a freak for sure.*

Although accustomed to his innate sixth sense popping up from time to time, Michael rarely told anyone when the hairs on the nape of his neck pricked his collar or when his stomach fluttered, signaling something looming the horizon. Most times it turned out to be nothing major, but other times his premonitions were dead on.

Once, his sophomore year in high school, he'd tossed and turned all night, unable to sleep. He had assumed the angst stemmed from stress over end of the year exams the following day. When he came home from school though, he had learned the real reason for the uneasy assault. His grandmother had passed away in the night.

From then on, Michael had paid close attention to those feelings of dread while secretly hoping it turned out to be the side effect of an overactive imagination. He hoped for the same this time.

Jared's brows pinched with notable curiosity. "What kind of feeling?"

"Nothin', man." Michael hopped up on the toilet and stared blindly out the window into the nothingness of the dark.

"I thought for a second you were gonna say some weird shit like you have premonitions or some other crazy-assed thing."

Michael glanced down at him and faked a smile. Blue eyes sparkled back in the fluorescent light.

Jared puffed on his cigarette again and cleared his throat. He stared at the opposite wall where Michael had stood. "I mean, if you did have some bad psychic feeling, maybe it wouldn't be so fucked up." Jared shrugged. "Hell, come to think of it, it may even be kinda cool, ya' know?"

Michael narrowed his gaze. Had Jared given him a pass on the weird psychic thing? He snorted a laugh. "Well if the world spirals out of orbit, don't say I didn't warn ya'."

Jared laughed. "Now wouldn't that be some shit?"

Michael stood over the other man, savoring every moment of uninterrupted privacy they shared in the cramped bathroom stall. He found himself intently drawn to the way Jared's lips turned up at the corners when he smiled. *Damn. He's sexy as hell.*

Michael looked down at his cigarette, already burned down to the filter. He let it fall from his fingers into the toilet bowl between his feet.

Jared leaned toward him, placed his hand on the toilet handle behind Michael's knees and simultaneously tossed his cigarette butt into the water as he flushed it. His head tilted upward, and the instant Michael met Jared's baby-blue orbs, Michael's cock twitched, inches from Jared's face.

The intensity of the otherwise innocent look might have been nothing, but something clicked in Michael's mind. Something familiar. Something he'd longed to see, but never imagined he ever would. Was Jared into him, too?

A long, awkward silence passed between them until Michael decided to hop down from his perch, but as his boot left the rim of the toilet, he lost his balance and slipped.

Strong hands grasped Michael's upper arm, and Jared grunted as he caught him.

Michael's face burned from the mere touch. The musky scent of aftershave mixed with a little sweat and smoke filled his nostrils. *He smells good, too.*

Jared cleared his throat and released his hold. "You okay, kid?"

Michael tried to hide his heated glare as he heard the word "*kid*" once again. He bit the flesh on the inside of his cheek to keep from saying what he wanted to say. *I got your kid right here, Prophet.*

"Yeah, I'm good." Michael pulled away, straightened his shirt and reached for the door.

A firm grip caught his forearm, and Michael's attention snapped back to Jared, then down to where the other man held his arm.

Jared looked down, too, then quickly released him and ran his fingers through his hair. "Hey, um, where are you from anyway?" His Adam's apple bobbed up and down.

Small talk? Okay. "DFW."

A crooked smile spread across Jared's lips, those oh so kissable lips. "Dallas, huh?" He snorted. "I'm from down around Houston." His shoulders seemed to shrink, and his blue eyes darkened as the mood in their impromptu hideaway took on a solemn air. "It's nice to know there's another Texan around. You know? Someone who understands the way we think. The way we're raised here in the south."

Michael shook his head. "Um, I'm not following."

Jared's cheeks flushed bright red. "You know? Someone from up north or the west coast may get the wrong idea about the two of us in this stall… at night…alone…"

Is that right? Michael wondered if people would automatically jump to conclusions, or had Jared revealed his biggest fear without even realizing it?

What better time to find out? Michael squared his shoulders, suddenly feeling two feet taller than he had when he first walked into the bathroom. He leaned into Jared and purposefully inhaled slow and deep, savoring the man's scent while subtly inching Jared against the wall behind them. "Anyone with brains would know right away what this is."

Jared's eyes widened, and all color drained from his cheeks. "And wh-what is that?"

Michael eased even closer, placing his mouth millimeters from Jared's ear. His breathing steadied as Jared seemed to stop breathing altogether.

Anger and possibly even disgust fueled Michael's intimidating demeanor. He wouldn't allow anyone, not even Jared Prophet, make him feel ashamed of who he was. "Two grown-ass men having a smoke." Michael pounded the wall then pushed open the stall door.

He'd made it halfway across the room when he heard Jared's grumbled, "Shit!"

Michael smiled. Just because Jared Prophet swung his bat on the down-low, didn't mean he and Michael weren't playing for the same team.

"Hey," Jared called out as he stepped from the stall. "What's your name, Private?"

Michael hid his satisfied grin before turning around as he opened the bathroom door. "Michael Crest, but I have a feeling you already knew that, didn't you?"

Chapter Two

Jared Prophet tried his best not to show Private Crest his true self. He'd safely tucked away those dark feelings for years. He'd never allow some guy to come along and change his decision to keep his secret desires in check.

Growing up in a small, conservative southern community on the outskirts of Houston, Jared would be shunned as though he had leprosy and his parents would disown him if they knew his true nature. He'd fought a life-long battle, nothing less than a curse, within himself, and he'd be damned if he'd act on it now. He had too much to lose.

"Thanks again for the smokes. I owe ya' one."

Michael smiled and chuckled. "Actually you owe me two, but who's counting?"

Jared clutched the small Marlboro box still in his hand, remembering the one remaining cigarette left in the pack. "Two then."

"No problem." Michael turned on his heel and disappeared through the bathroom door leaving Jared behind.

Jared breathed a sigh of relief and headed straight to the sink to splash cold water on his face. He hadn't spoken much to the young private before the all too brief encounter, but Jared had noticed him the first day Michael arrived on base.

He recalled the deep dimples digging into Michael's cheeks when he smiled. The baritone timber of his voice, as smooth and steady as the man himself and one of the first things about Michael to snag Jared's attention. Michael exuded confidence. Confidence one possessed from being comfortable in his own skin, sure of who he was and not at all afraid to show it. If only

Jared were able to be as free with his own feelings.

As he raised his head, Jared caught a glimpse of his reflection in the mirror. His cheeks reddened, and his heart boomed in his chest at the thought of how attractive he found the other man. *What the fuck?*

"Stop it," he growled under his breath.

Jared smoothed a shaky hand over the side of his head, slicking down his crew-cut to make sure he looked every bit the soldier he'd striven to be: proud, strong, and every inch a red-blooded American man. The man his father wanted him to be, the man *he* needed to be to survive.

He only had to get through another few weeks. By then his retirement papers would be approved, allowing him to start over somewhere, anywhere, as a civilian.

"Man, the wind is crazy," someone spoke behind him as they entered the bathroom.

Jared turned off the water and peered back in the mirror at Raul Arrozo.

"Good thing you know how to swim, *mojado*," Jared said.

"*Mojado?* Man, I keep tellin' ya'. My pops didn't swim across the border. He was smuggled into this country under your mama's fat ass."

"Prick."

"Douche."

Both men squared off in the center of the bathroom, scowling at one another with jaws clenched taut. Jared sized him up with a piercing glare. Rather small in stature, Raul stood only five feet six inches or so. Broad across the shoulders, built like a Mexican bulldog and every bit as ugly.

Jared could take him if he had to.

The room grew quiet, and the air instantly thickened.

Raul's jaw tightened. He wasn't backing down, and he didn't have to.

Jared gave in first. "For the record, my mama's ass ain't that fat."

Raul laughed aloud and slapped Jared's back. "I know. I smacked it last night."

"You are not right in the head." Jared tried his best not to laugh and headed for the door.

"Hey, what are you doin' for block leave?"

"I only have two weeks, so I guess it'll depend on how bad this weather is. If it blows over, I'll head home for a few days or maybe up to my parent's lake-house for some fishin'. With any luck, I'll miss the tropical storm altogether."

"Aw, man. That sounds like the perfect R an' R. I haven't been fishin' since I was twelve. We didn't exactly have a lot of lakes where I grew up in New Mexico. A lot of cactus though." Raul stood in front of the urinal and unzipped his pants.

Jared's face heated. A sudden burst of embarrassment rippled through him as Raul pissed right in front of him, fresh on the heels of the erotic thoughts he'd had about Michael Crest. *What the fuck's wrong with me?*

Jared cleared his throat and grabbed the door handle. He wanted nothing more than to get the hell out of the bathroom, but he had to keep his cool. After all, he and Raul were friends. "Well, maybe we should meet up there and try to catch a few before our leave is up."

Raul zipped his zipper and reached for the soap dispenser by the sink. "Great idea. I might even bring a couple smokin' hot ladies and make a real party out of it, eh *ese*?"

Jared nodded with forced enthusiasm. "Now you're talkin'."

"Well, give me a shout out when you're ready, and I'll bring the party favors." A goofy grin spread across Raul's face, and Jared couldn't help but laugh at his friend.

"Sounds like a plan." Jared left the bathroom and rushed out into the stormy night, if only to put some distance between himself and the thought of Raul actually following through with the plans to bring girls up to the lake-house for a little casual sex.

Then again, the thought of a soft, curvy, sweet-smelling woman would probably be exactly what Jared needed to take his mind off of Michael Crest.

Jared lowered his head and trotted across the parking lot to his car. He needed to get to the one person who would always be up for a little mind-blowing fun. *Tiffany.*

Tiffany, if that was even her real name, danced at the Puss-N-Boots strip club on the weekends, and if Jared hurried, he may be able to offer her a ride home.

He had a few hours before he had to report back, so if he was going to cleanse his system of thoughts he dared not acknowledge, now was his chance.
****

Jared pulled into the parking lot of the strip club and parked off to the side, making sure his car was out of view from the street. Turning up the collar of his windbreaker, he made a mad dash for the front doors.

The dark foyer reeked of smoke and a mixture of cheap cologne and liquor. As he entered the club, his attention was immediately drawn to center stage. One of the newer dancers squatted in front of a patron as he tucked money into her thong. Her breasts, larger than most, were quite firm for their size, and her erect nipples indicated she enjoyed her job as much as the men who admired her.

Golden glitter sparkled down the length of her legs, and she ran her fingers across her flesh, caressing her skin, shamelessly teasing her patrons. Her body glistened like melted caramel as she tilted her head back and squeezed her breasts together, then playfully plucked her nipple while giving her lips the once over with the tip of her tongue. Multitasking.

Jared eased closer, fascinated by the woman's ability to turn her body into a work of modern art, twisting and contorting around the pole placed at the end of the stage. With one hand stretched above her head, she gripped the pole and slipped her other hand inside the front of her thong, giving the illusion of masturbating, much to the delight of the cavemen in the front row, who salivated over her every move.

As if he had room to talk. He was there for the same reason as the other men. To watch. Admire. Fantasize. And with any luck, find Tiffany and prove how much of a man he truly was.

Tiffany had been his remedy for those times he found his mind wandering to thoughts he knew he shouldn't have. Michael Crest wasn't the first man to stir up ideas and feelings Jared knew better than to give into.

Jared sat back as the music poured over him. Each boom of the bass drilled deeper and deeper into his head.

The lights dimmed, and another dancer took center stage. When the lights came back up, Sasha, one of Tiffany's friends, stood before him dressed in mock army fatigues. She didn't look like any of the female personnel on base with her flaming red hair, perky breasts and legs stretching on forever. The heels she wore only made her statuesque figure more desirable.

That proved it, didn't it? He couldn't possibly be in to Michael Crest or any other guy for that matter. Not if he was this attracted to women.

Whatever those other thoughts were, it didn't mean he was gay.

Sarah, one of the waitresses, quite the looker herself, slipped up beside him to take his drink order. She ran warm fingers across the back of his neck, gently caressing his hair, as he focused on Sasha doing her thing on stage.

Sarah leaned in and whispered in his ear, "What can I get ya' tonight, lover boy?"

He glanced up at her. "Bud Light and Tiffany, if she's here."

Sarah winked. "Good choices. I'll tell her you're waiting."

Jared watched the girl walk away, then quickly returned his attention to Sasha. He tried to concentrate on her eyes. Something about the eyes always got to him before anything else. His gaze trailed down, and he licked his lips when she slowly unbuttoned her camouflage jacket. *See, there's nothing wrong. Women do it for you.*

"Hey there." Tiffany's voice echoed in his ear.

Jared immediately got to his feet to greet her. Old habits were hard to break when a woman approached, even in a strip club where most men probably wouldn't bother. "Tiffany," he said, heat singeing his cheeks.

"Private dance?" She wagged her eyebrows as she nudged him backward and slipped onto his lap.

Jared's heart raced. "In the back?" He fought the urge to touch. He knew better, at least not in the main room of the club. The back rooms were a different story. Away from the crowd, private dances were known to get a bit more personal.

Tiffany smiled. "Sure, lover."

Jared rose and followed her toward the back of the club, casting one last glance back at Sasha who had wrapped one leg around the pole, giving the guys on the front row a peek of what was hidden under her camo bikini bottoms.

The rooms at the back weren't completely private with closed doors, but rather a circular booth tucked into a cubbyhole, with a thick row of hanging bead-strands serving as a semi-see-through doorway. The lights were much dimmer and the music a bit lower, providing the perfect atmosphere for dancers to talk dirty to the customers.

If anything sexual happened there, no one could see, and naturally no one said anything one way or the other. After all, the girls were entertainers, not prostitutes, and not all dancers gave private shows.

"How you been, baby?" Tiffany asked as she guided him into the booth.

"Good. How about you?" Jared looked up at her as she straddled him.

Her blonde hair cascaded across her shoulders, and she began to grind into his crotch. She truly was beautiful. Far too beautiful to be a stripper. Such a waste.

"I'm much better now that I have you to play with."

The girl had skills. No denying it. Jared grinned, pretending to buy into her bullshit. "This is exactly what I've needed all week." He slid his hand up her thigh.

Tiffany placed her hand on top of his and guided it to his leg. "I'm more interested in what you're packin' there, soldier."

Her hand pushed toward his groin, and in a few seconds she stroked his cock through his jeans.

Chills ricocheted across his body, and he tilted his head back and closed his eyes. "Mmm, feels nice."

Tiffany's hot breath spilled onto his neck. "I wanna fuck you so bad."

"So fuck me."

"Not here. You know the rules."

"Then where?"

"After work."

Jared pulled out his wallet and held up a hundred dollar bill. "Then give me something to tide me over until then."

"You don't need to pay me, baby."

"I know, but if you're over here with me, you're not out there making tips." It wasn't the first time he'd tipped her for something he knew she would give him for free. But he was right; she had bills to pay, and she would definitely earn it.

"Stick it in." Tiffany rose up and thrust her pelvis toward him.

Jared slowly stuck the bill down the front of her thong. Taking advantage of the low lighting, he cupped her shaved mound, then dipped one finger into her slit, making sure to graze her clit as he pulled his hand out.

"Oh, you're in for it now." Soft kisses followed as she snuggled close, rubbing her breasts against his chest.

Jared could play this game all night. Whatever it took to get off and whatever it took to keep his mind where it needed to be.

He leaned his head back again and allowed Tiffany to perform her exotic dance, which consisted mostly of a slow grind and the occasional dick massage.

Closing his eyes, he pictured soft lips wrapped around his hard cock. He imagined the deep, erotic moans of pleasure echoing through his mind. Exactly what he wanted, what he needed to relieve himself of those other thoughts, the thoughts capable of destroying him.

Jared concentrated as Tiffany writhed in his lap, coaxing his erection to grow even harder.

He imagined the feel of his prick buried deep

inside her warm mouth, wet lips gliding up and down the length of him. In his mind, he ran his fingers through her hair, thrusting himself upwards into her mouth, deeper until he touched the back of her throat.

Jared then pictured himself watching her and how he would wait to come, wait until he saw those eyes and then… when he couldn't hold it anymore… he'd lift her chin and – Michael Crest's face appeared in his mind's eye, sporting a cunning smile and glistening lips.

Jared's eyelids sprang open, and he jerked away from Tiffany. His heart pounded to a near painful level. "Fuck!"

Tiffany jumped back. "Babe, are you okay?" Her eyes widened, and he knew instantly he'd startled her.

He scrambled to clear his mind and gain his bearings. "Yeah, I, uh, it's been a long day. I think I'm tired."

"We can do this another time. You know I'm always here for you."

"Yeah, I know. I'll get a little sleep, and then I'll be good as new." He shifted her off of his lap, stood and straightened his clothing. "I'll call you, okay?"

Tiffany reached for his hand. "Jared, if you need to talk, I'll be home around three."

"Zero three hundred, got it." He repeated it back to her in military time.

She rose up from the booth and kissed his cheek. "I mean it," she whispered in his ear.

Jared gazed down at the stunning girl. How many times had they had sex? Judging from the way she looked at him, perhaps one time too many. Her eyes hinted to the notion there might be something more on her mind than sex when she thought of him. *Great. Now I've fucked her up, too.*

Jared swiped her chin with the knuckle of his bent

finger. "I know."

Tiffany pulled the hundred dollar bill from the band of her thong. "Here." She pressed it to his chest.

Jared placed his hand over hers and squeezed, causing the bill to crumple in her fingers. "You keep it."

"But I—"

"You earned it, Tiffany. Trust me, you earned it." He gave her hand another gentle squeeze and left her standing there.

The wind still hadn't let up, and when he finally reached his car, Jared sat there for a few moments until the burn behind his eyes nearly gave way to tears. He gripped the steering wheel so tightly his knuckles flared white. One way or another he'd get the thoughts of Michael Crest, and every other man who had ever snagged his attention, out of his head. He would purge the thoughts, no matter what it took.

Chapter Three

Michael hadn't slept as much as he'd planned, so when the alarm went off at zero four hundred hours, he had barely fallen asleep. He hit the snooze button three times before he finally got up, dressed and headed out to begin morning PT.

The storm had passed, and though the ground was wet, a little mud wouldn't stop the strict routine of Army physical training. After a few stretches and some much needed stress relieving calisthenics, Michael was set for a good run. He'd get in a couple of miles before breakfast, then go back to his apartment, pack and get out of town before all hell broke loose.

He ran down the path toward the thickest part of the woods behind the base. He preferred this part of the trail because it was quiet and gave him time to think without a lot of traffic crowding him. Today, he figured everyone else would be avoiding the woods because of the previous night's storm. There were bound to be fallen limbs or even trees and definitely some mud and muck to hinder the easy flow of the trail, but Michael appreciated the challenge.

He'd barely hit his stride when Jared Prophet's face invaded the quiet solitude of his thoughts. There had to be something more to the way Jared acted around him. Michael didn't know much about him, other than he was sexy and not much of a talker. Jared kept to himself a lot, and the friends they had in common never mentioned him at all.

This intrigued Michael the most. How could a man live in such close proximity to so many fellow soldiers and not come up in conversation? Jared was well liked from what he saw while interacting within the same circles. Being medics, Michael had crossed Jared's path, though they rarely worked the same department or shift.

Michael worked at the clinic on base, handling everything from sprained ankles to ear aches, while Jared handled emergency first-aid and trauma training drills for new recruits. Jared was also one of the few guys he'd met who'd seen actual combat. Michael had yet to be deployed, though it was simply a matter of time.

Michael tried not to dwell on those aspects of being in the army. He knew why he enlisted and would do what had to be done when his country called for him. In the meantime, he did his job and made sure he took good care of his fellow soldiers while on base.

The thought of Jared in danger, getting shot, killing or being killed hadn't been anything Michael considered before, but as his attraction grew, how would he keep from thinking about all the shit that might go wrong?

Michael shook it off and picked up his pace. *Don't put the cart before the horse. Jared Prophet may not even be into me at all.*

Why worry about negative outcomes over a gut feeling? True, there had been that little sparkle in Jared's eye, but even that might have been wishful thinking.

Michael continued his run and allowed the scattered thoughts in his mind to settle as he made his way deeper into the forest where the trail branched off. One path led around a small lake then circled around, and the other led straight back to the base.

Checking his watch and seeing he still had plenty of time before chow, Michael chose the longer path.

The sun rose on the opposite side of the small lake. The wind died down to practically nothing, so the water appeared as smooth as glass where the first golden rays of morning light reflected off the surface. Absolute peace.

Michael paused and pressed his palms into his knees as he bent over to catch his breath. The sounds of nature echoed across the open lake with soft chirps and whistles from birds waking to the new day. The rustling of a bush on the edge of the water hinted other creatures were awakening, as well. Michael relished the subtleties of life as it existed here, the way nature intended.

He'd wished countless times for his life to be so simple. To wake and greet the day exactly the way he was meant to. To innately know what was expected and then do it without second thought. How easy was that?

Why had it been the opposite for him? Why couldn't he have been like everyone else he knew as a kid and wake up to a nice girl asleep in his arms?

Michael already knew the answer. In fact, he'd known for sure since he was fifteen years old. Peering across the lake reminded him of the exact moment he first knew without a doubt he was different.

He remembered it as though it were yesterday. Standing on the edge of the riverbank down the road from his house, Jennifer Mullins had kissed him, and it hadn't been a simple a peck on the cheek. No, the full-on *French kiss* had changed his life forever.

Every boy in the neighborhood would have sold their grandmother's soul for the same opportunity, but all Michael thought while her lips were fused to his, was whether or not her brother, Jake, would ever get up the nerve to kiss him like that.

The two boys had spent a lot of time together that summer, and their campouts had been filled by an easiness neither felt the need to mention to the other. Jake had even held Michael's hand as they lay in their tent talking about sports and what they wanted to do when they grew up. Michael knew how it felt to love someone. It came as naturally as any other feeling he had ever known.

Michael had even gone so far as to purposefully lean into Jake when private moments passed between them, but Jake had only stared at him for a long moment then backed away and changed the subject. Michael knew the other boy felt the same, but Jake had always chickened out at the last possible second.

Jake finally had acted on their mutual attraction when Michael was seventeen. A year older than Michael, Jake had been about to leave for college and had asked Michael to meet him behind his house.

Michael had leaned against a tree and listened to Jake go on and on about how the world worked and how they had a responsibility to their families and their friends. He had told Michael that the time they'd spent together were memories he'd secretly treasure, but they would never be together.

After nearly three years of anticipation, Jake had only mustered enough courage for a hit and run kiss that was over before Michael even realized it had happened. He was left there leaning against the big oak tree in Jake's backyard, with a hard-on from hell and a desperate desire to feel that way again as often as possible.

In the three years since that night, Michael had had a couple of chances to do more than kiss, but it never felt like the right time or the right guy. Something always stopped him from going all the way. Now though, he wanted nothing more than an opportunity to be himself and allow that kind of love to happen. Was Jared Prophet the one?

The loud sound of a cracking tree branch startled Michael and interrupted his reminiscent train of thought. He swung around. "Shit, you scared me."

Jared stepped out from the darkened tree line. "I didn't know anyone was here."

Michael sucked in a deep breath to settle his rattled nerves. "No problem. I thought I was alone, too."

Jared kicked at a pinecone on the ground in front of him. "Sorry to interrupt." He turned on his heel and headed back the way he came.

Panic surged through Michael at the thought of Jared leaving. "You don't have to go."

Jared stopped, but remained facing the trees. He didn't say anything. He stood there as if frozen in place.

"It's a great day for a run, don't ya' think?"

Jared slowly pivoted back into Michael's direction. "Yeah, it's okay."

"I'm finishing up then heading back to pack up for leave."

Jared nodded, but still had no reply.

"You headin' out of town, too?"

Jared narrowed his gaze as though bothered by the conversation.

Michael's heart raced, and his palms began to perspire as the space between them adopted an uncomfortable air as it so often did. "Well, I guess I'll see you around." Michael drew in a deep breath and took off at a slow jog.

A few moments later, Jared sidled up beside him, his stride even with Michael's.

"I don't talk much." Jared finally spoke.

"I noticed."

"I don't make friends easily."

Curiosity dug in. "Why's that?"

Jared slowed and fell back.

Michael stopped running and jogged in place as he watched Jared, wondering what was going through his mind.

"Look, I'm not trying to be a dick. I appreciate the smokes last night, and I know you're only trying to be nice, but I'm not here to make friends. I'm here to do my job and hopefully go home feet first. I don't need distractions."

Michael chewed the inside of his cheek as he contemplated the possible meaning behind Jared's words. "Distractions?"

"Friends, okay? Buddies." Jared folded his arms across his chest. "I don't socialize much."

"Cool," Michael said. "I get it."

Jared stared at the ground between them. "Okay."

"Okay, well if you don't mind, I'd really like to get another mile in before breakfast." Michael turned back and headed down the trail, secretly hoping to hear Jared behind him.

In a matter of seconds, the sound of plodding footsteps came closer, and it wasn't long before Jared appeared in Michael's peripheral vision. Michael refrained from acknowledging him, fearing the unwanted attention would push him away. Maybe Jared liked him more than he'd hoped. After all, he hadn't turned around and headed back to the barracks.

For now, Michael was content to be near him, even if that meant not talking.

As they headed over a steep hill on the far side of the lake, the terrain took an unexpected turn. Clay mud, camouflaged by loose pine needles, hid a dangerous, slippery slope created from all the recent rain. As they reached the peak and began down the opposite side, Michael's foot bogged down in the mud, and in an instant he tumbled head over heels down the hill.

When Jared's grunts and groans echoed around him, Michael realized Jared had immediately taken the same painful way down the hill to the bottom.

A sharp pain jabbed into Michael's side as his body came to an abrupt halt against a large pine tree.

"Fuck!" His body recoiled, and he cradled his abdomen. "I think I cracked a rib."

"Holy shit." Jared chortled from only a few feet away. "That was almost as much fun as the mud slides we made in the neighborhood ditches after a good rain when I was a kid."

Michael eased up onto his elbow, painfully mindful of his probable injury. "I'm glad my busted ribs are amusing."

Jared rose on all fours and crawled over to Michael, stifling his laugh. "I doubt they're broken, but I'll check them out to make sure, then get you back to the infirmary."

"Nah, that's okay. I'll be okay."

Jared knelt before Michael, towering over him.

As Michael looked up, the morning sun radiated over Jared's head, and a surge of warmth ricocheted across Michael's skin.

"If they're broken and you move the wrong—"

"I know, I know. It could puncture my lung."

Jared cracked a smile. "Right, so take off your shirt, and let's take a look."

Michael's heart raced as he managed to fight through the blast of pain and sat up. He leaned against the giant tree that had stopped his fall and braced for the uncomfortable moments he knew were about to occur.

Jared waited, his gaze fixed on Michael's hands.

Michael figured Jared would turn away or say something as he lifted his t-shirt up over his torso, but instead, Jared's hands trembled as he reached down and helped Michael draw it over his head without saying a word.

The forest suddenly became eerily still.

Michael glared up at Jared, half expecting him to disappear. He bit his tongue, holding back any sound capable of breaking the spell Jared seemed to have fallen under.

Jared eased closer, still on his knees and slowly lifted the bottom of Michael's wife-beater, then pulled it up and over his head. For a few intense seconds, Michael sat before him, his bare chest about to explode from his heart pounding furiously inside.

Jared licked his lips and moved toward Michael, as if in slow motion, until the palms of his hands were flush against Michael's chest. Michael's nipple beaded as Jared's fingers lightly skimmed over his flesh.

It was then that Jared finally looked Michael in the eyes, and Michael held his breath as a silent conversation passed between them.

Jared's jaw flexed taut, and he lowered his head so slowly, Michael was sure he would lose his mind from the sheer thrill of anticipation. He'd forgotten all about the pain, and Jared was definitely not examining his ribs.

Michael lifted his chin, and before he knew it, Jared's lips grazed his.

Jared snapped back as though he'd been zapped by lightning. His bright blue eyes smoldered, and then he closed them and pressed his mouth to Michael's once again. This time though, he didn't stop.

Michael acted on desires he'd hidden for weeks and moved his hand behind Jared's head, drawing him even closer. His tongue plunged in deep, and his cock hardened at the sound of Jared's deep moan.

Jared pulled him in tighter and kissed him harder, so hard their teeth clanked together sending a little twinge of discomfort shooting across Michael's gums. The faint metallic taste of blood filled his mouth, but he ignored it. Nothing was going to interrupt.

He struggled to breathe as Jared's hands began to wander. He reached down and grabbed Michael's hand

and without hesitation planted it right across his cock. The long, thick shaft bulged behind Jared's zipper, and Michael struggled to contain his delight.

Jared rose, towering over Michael like a god demanding adoration.

Michael had never done this, but he'd never wanted anything more. He fumbled with Jared's zipper and unfastened his pants, panting like a kid in a candy store as he freed his prize.

Jared clasped Michael's shoulders then, nudging him back, his eyes widened, and a look of sheer panic flashed across Jared's face. "So help me, if you ever tell—"

"I-I won't. I swear."

Jared cupped the back of Michael's neck and brought his head toward Jared's crotch.

Michael leaned in to the swollen prick pulsating in his hand. The instant his lips touched the bulbous tip, the salty-sweet taste of pre-cum filled his mouth, and Jared's entire body seized under Michael's touch.

Unsure of what to do exactly, Michael followed his instincts and eased the heated shaft deeper into his mouth, then began to slide it in and out, leaving behind saliva mixed with Jared's juices up and down his cock. His sensitive tongue caressed the deep, pulsing veins on the underside of the shaft, encouraging his own cock to swell in his pants.

Jared grunted. "Fuck! That feels good." He rubbed the back of Michael's head.

Michael tuned him out and concentrated on sucking even harder and faster until his hollowed cheeks were dampened from the tasty juices seeping from Jared's cock.

Jared's breathing increased. "I'm gonna come," he said between pants.

The sound of those words excited Michael to the point of explosion. He slid his hand toward the base of Jared's shaft and began to stroke him.

Michael looked up, and Jared glared through hooded eyes with a look of sheer ecstasy on his face. Michael ran his tongue over the tip as he jerked him off, staring up at Jared the whole time.

Jared opened his mouth, and his breathing became even more labored. He moved Michael's hand and mouth away and began to stroke his own cock, then bent over and kissed Michael, still holding him by the nape of his neck with his other hand.

A warm sensation shot across Michael's bare chest as Jared came, and then, as though he'd lost all energy, he leaned onto Michael. Jared's heavy panting filled the air with huffs of satisfied release.

Michael wasn't sure how long they lingered there in the quiet dawn, but he was sure he'd never forget a second of what had occurred. He'd given his first blow-job, and it was with Jared Prophet of all people.

Jared fidgeted and stepped back. "I'm sorry." He crammed his dick back inside his pants then helped Michael to his feet. "That shouldn't have happened."

Michael reached for him. "It's okay, I—"

Jared jerked away. "No, I shouldn't have – *we* shouldn't have…"

A surge of nausea bubbled in Michael's gut. "It's cool, man." It wasn't cool at all, but he wasn't about to be a bitch about it or let Jared ruin it for him.

Jared glanced over at him, then reached in his back pocket and pulled out a pack of Marlboro Reds. "Want one?"

Michael shook his head, struggling to keep the hot, acidic bile in the back of his throat from gagging him.

Jared lit a cigarette and stood there silently once again.

Is he really going to pretend this didn't happen? "Look, I have to pack, so I better get back."

"Uh, yeah, sure." Jared stared at the muddy earth beneath them. "Make sure you go by the infirmary and have those ribs checked out."

Michael glared at Jared with an infuriating urge to knock the shit out of him. "Don't worry about it. I'm fine." He cradled his now throbbing side and bent down to retrieve his clothes. "Fuck." Michael winced as a dizzying pain shot through his chest.

Jared immediately grabbed him, preventing him from toppling over into the mud. "I got ya'." He stomped out his cigarette, took Michael's shirt and undershirt and slung them over his shoulder along with Michael's arm.

Michael held his breath for no other reason than to disguise the pain, not wanting to appear weak in Jared's eyes.

Jared guided him up the embankment and then around the lake in the direction of base. Neither man said a word.

Michael ignored the pleasure of being in Jared's arms. Having Jared help him back to base wasn't exactly romantic, but then again, sucking the guy's cock in the muddy woods wasn't exactly Michael's idea of a date either, but it was what it was.

When they reached the edge of the forest where the buildings came into view, Michael stopped. "I need my shirt back."

Jared released him and stood there for a second before handing them back. "Yeah, sure, man." He noticeably avoided eye contact.

Michael took his wife-beater and painstakingly pulled it over his head, but he did not put on his t-shirt.

There was no need. He'd only have to take it off again when he got to the infirmary anyway.

"Hey, I hope nothing's broken," Jared called out as Michael walked away.

Michael didn't reply. He kept his eyes set on the building across the field. He already knew what he'd see if he looked back. Shame and fear were expressions he'd seen the night Jake Mullins had kissed him goodbye behind his house.

Jared Prophet was as scared and fucked up as Jake had been, and Michael wasn't about to waste another minute of his life on a guy who wasn't man enough to admit who he was, who wasn't secure enough to be himself.

Fuck that!

If Jared liked Michael, then he would have to come to him. Michael damn sure wasn't about to chase him. The next two weeks' leave would provide some distance, and if Jared was still being a flake after they returned, then so be it. It was his loss.

Chapter Four

Jared watched Michael hobble off to the infirmary. He drew in a deep breath to curtail the sickening swill sloshing in his stomach. *What the fuck have I done?*

When Michael disappeared around the corner, Jared wanted so badly to follow. What was it about Michael Crest that gnawed at him so? Had he really allowed Michael to give him head as though it were nothing? As though it were an everyday occurrence? Who did things like that?

He made a beeline to his quarters, stripped down and stood under the hot flow of water in his shower. His mind ran wild with images, smells and even the taste of blood. Had they become so enthralled that he'd bitten Michael's lip, or had it happened when their teeth clanked together?

The passion was so intense, Jared had thought he would come all over the guy the instant Michael's fingers touched his cock.

Michael's slight build, smooth tanned skin and soft feminine-like features had managed to set swarms of uncontrollable flutters loose in Jared's stomach from the first time he'd laid eyes on the new recruit, long before what had happened between them in the woods.

The mere brush of Michael's arm against his caused Jared's whole body to tense and quake at the same time as if he'd been zapped by an electrical current. Jared also sensed Michael wanted more than he'd ever allow.

Jared wasn't unfamiliar with men gawking at him. His first sexual experience had been anything but pleasant when he was little more than a kid. Twelve, actually. Back then, he'd hated the feeling of being touched, looked at and coveted by a guy. It made him feel dirty, like he was doing something wrong, but at the same time his body reacted the way it had when he found himself with girls as an older teenager, confusing what his brain knew to be unnatural. Young kids weren't supposed to like being touched. His heart knew it was wrong, but what choice did he have? He was just a kid.

Up until now, Jared had ignored the natural desire he felt when someone like Michael Crest undressed him with those amazing brown eyes. Michael's gaze poured over him like cream over a bowl full of fresh strawberries, making him feel anything but dirty. In fact, it made him feel downright embarrassed at the thoughts that came to mind. Erotic, dangerous thoughts, far surpassing a blowjob in the woods.

Jared shook his head, fighting back tears. *I can't do this.*

One way or another he had to stay away from Michael, and he had to make sure Michael understood in the event he had ideas of picking up where they left off. Jared wouldn't fuck up everything he'd worked so hard to avoid because some guy wanted to continue a little game of slap and tickle.

Jared balled his hands into tight fists at his side and dug his nails into his palms to break the wandering thoughts of something so forbidden, something so wrong. A little self-inflicted pain always did the trick.

He pressed his forehead against the shower wall and allowed the hot water to stream down his back. Restless thoughts plagued his mind. How did this happen? What if Michael told someone? What if someone saw them? What if Michael wanted to— *No!* He had to stop thinking about Michael. He had to keep himself on track.

Jared turned off the water, stepped out of the shower and wrapped a towel around his waist. He pulled another from the towel rack and began to dry his hair and torso. Swiping the towel across the mirror, Jared stared at his reflection. "You have to stop this," he told himself. "You'll lose everything if you don't."

Entering the living room of the efficiency style apartment in his barrack's building, he headed for the kitchen for a beer. As he passed the bar separating the two small rooms, his cell phone buzzed on the counter.

Jared glanced down at Arrozo's number flashing on the LCD screen and answered it. "Hello?"

"Dude, are we still on for the lake-house thing?"

Jared took a deep breath. Raul and a couple of girls would probably get him back on track. What would it hurt to have a little fun? "Yeah, man. I think we should do it up right."

"Cool. Text me the address, and I'll look it up on the GPS."

"Great. I'll send it now."

"Hey, do you mind if we add a couple people to the party?"

Jared scratched his head. "Nah, I don't mind, but don't invite the whole damn base. The place isn't a mansion."

Raul laughed on the other end of the line. "No problem, just a couple of my buddies and the girls. They got beer."

"Okay, that's cool."

"See ya'."

"Later, man." Jared hung up and immediately sent the address via text. Now all he had to do was pack some clothes, buy some beer and food, fill his gas tank, and get the hell out of Dodge.

He grabbed a beer and drank it down as he packed his duffel bag. Before he left his bedroom, he opened the top drawer of his nightstand and pulled out a box of condoms then tossed them in the bag with his clothes. *All set*. He'd definitely get his shit together over the next two weeks, and Michael Crest would be permanently erased from his memory.

****

Jared stopped at a small gas station a mile or so away from the lake-house road. He hadn't been there in a while, so he was glad it was still in business. Everything looked pretty much as he'd remembered when he walked inside.

Cool air flooded over him as he passed under the air conditioner on the back wall by the soda and beer refrigeration unit, reminding him of hot summer days when he was a child.

His dad, a particularly stern man, had never allowed him to run wild in the store the way his cousins had. Jared had always wanted to dive into the ice cream bin the way his uncle let his kids, but his dad wouldn't hear of it. No child of Jonathan Prophet would be caught dead running amuck like a heathen.

As Jared approached the ice cream, he paused and peered through the sliding glass lid at the rows of popsicles, fudge bars and ice cream. Glancing around to see if anyone was watching, he slowly pushed the lid open. A burst of freezing mist blew out and into his face as he leaned over. He reached in and pulled out a handful of frozen treats.

Quite pleased, he shoved them into a hand held basket stacked on the back of the bin and moved onto the next items on his mental list. Seventy-five dollars later, Jared had bought enough beer and junk food to feed a small army, well, his army anyway.

Loaded down, Jared drove the remaining short distance to his family's lake-house.

When he pulled into the drive, Arrozo's pickup

truck was already there, along with a newer model black Dodge Charger. *Nice ride.* He wondered who it belonged to. He hadn't recalled seeing it around base, but then again, he didn't know everyone.

Raul sat on the tailgate with a petite brunette positioned between his legs. They cuddled and kissed as Jared exited his car. "I see you found the place okay."

"Yup, I Googled," Raul said as he jumped off the tailgate. He stopped, turned to the girl, and then as if she weighed nothing at all, he picked her up and plopped her back down where he had sat.

Her giggles echoed across the property, and she pulled him toward her by his shirt collar and kissed him hard.

Jared shook his head. How had a guy like Raul managed to find a girl so pretty and then get her to kiss him – and *want* to? Raul wasn't downright ugly, but comparing him to a bulldog was about as accurate a description as it gets. He had a wide jaw and a slight under-bite. Acne scars had left pock marks over most of his face, and it damn sure wouldn't have hurt him to lose a few pounds. How he'd managed to keep a beer gut with all the exercise they did was beyond Jared's ability to comprehend.

Raul tuned around, his cheeks bright red, and as if he'd read Jared's mind he smiled and said, "I know what you're thinking, and you're right. I have a big dick."

Jared laughed. "Dude, I've seen your dick, and trust me, it may be big by New Mexico standards, but it has nothing on a Texan."

"Oh, it's like that, huh, *ese*?"

Jared lifted a case of beer from the backseat and chortled. "Yeah, it's like that, *ese*."

Raul slapped him on the back. "Dude, I'd prove you wrong, but we're in mixed company, so for the sake of the ladies' delicate senses, I'll spare you the embarrassment."

"You do that." Jared nodded and grinned.

"Baby, I'm gonna help Jared get this stuff in the house. Why don't you go find Alana and everyone at the pier? You ladies can put on your bikinis and give us a show."

"Sure thing, papi." She smiled and hopped off the tailgate. "Thanks for inviting us, Jared. The lake is beautiful."

"Shit, I'm sorry, dude. This is April, my one and only." Raul pulled her to him and kissed the top of her head. Raul wasn't a very tall guy to begin with, and to say April stood more than five foot three would have been generous, but they did look as though they were made for each other.

"Nice to meet you, April."

April shook his hand and winked. "Better be careful, baby, I have a weakness for tall, handsome men."

Raul puffed his chest out. "I ain't worried about this gringo. I can kick his ass, and he knows it."

Jared laughed again. "That's right, April. Mad-dog here would break me in half. Then again, if he did that, both halves would still be taller than him, so I'd probably tag team him and win."

"Ha! You're a comedian now I see."

"Help me get this shit inside so we can start the party, would ya'?"

Raul grabbed a couple of bags and followed behind.

Jared unlocked the door, and they went into the house. Hot air assaulted them immediately. "We better open some windows and turn on some fans, then turn the air conditioner on after we air it out a bit." A musty odor permeated the house. It hadn't been opened up in quite some time. "I don't think my folks have made it up here in the last few months."

Raul began to open windows, and Jared emptied the grocery bags onto the counter and into the refrigerator. After all the beer had been loaded onto the shelves, it left little room for food. Good thing he'd only bought lunch meat and hot dog stuff.

From the living room, Jared heard more voices echo. April and her friends must have made it up from the pier. Jared shut the door and headed in to meet the girls. "Hey, we may need more—" Jared froze dead in his tracks.

"Jared, this is my friend Alana, her boyfriend Joel and his roommate, Michael," April said.

Jared's attention locked onto Michael's big brown eyes, and Jared swallowed hard, unable to speak. *Fuck, fuck, fuck!*

April's brows arched high. "Two other girls said they were coming, but one had to work and the other had to keep her sister's baby overnight for some emergency thing. I hope you don't mind."

"Uh, no. It's okay." Jared shoved his hands into his jeans pockets.

"More attention for you two lovely ladies," Raul said.

"Yeah." Joel draped his arm around Alana's shoulder.

Jared forced a smile. "Uh, we have three bedrooms, and the couch makes out into a bed. I guess I'll take my parents' room, and you four can divvy the other rooms." Jared glanced over at Michael. "Michael, right?"

Michael nodded with one brow slightly cocked upward.

"Um, I guess you can have the sofa bed."

"Right now, all I need is a restroom." Alana hopped from one foot to the other. "We haven't seen a decent public bathroom in two hours."

"Sure, follow me." Jared gestured toward the hallway.

He eyed Michael as he walked past leading Alana to the bathroom. "It's at the end of the hall." He entered before her. "Let me make sure there are no spiders in the toilet."

Alana jumped back with a shriek. "Spiders?"

He laughed. "Yeah, they tend to come and go as they please with the place empty most of the year."

She watched his every move as he checked the lid, tank and finally the bowl. "All clear, ma'am." Jared stepped back and opened the cabinet under the sink. "Everything you need is under here. Please, make yourself at home."

Alana cautiously entered the bathroom, and Jared turned and left the room, closing the door behind him.

As he pulled the door to, he looked up to find Michael coming toward him. Jared balled his fists, struggling to remain calm. He'd walked into his very own private kind of hell, and Michael Crest paved the way.

"Do you mind if I leave my stuff in a closet or something?"

Jared looked down at Michael's duffel bag. "Sure, man. You can leave it in my…uh… in this room." A cold sweat dotted his forehead and upper lip. He reached for the knob to his parents' bedroom.

Michel followed him inside. "Nice place."

"Thanks."

"You come here often?" Michael chuckled. "That wasn't a pick up line, by the way."

Jared glared at him, debating if he should laugh off the flirtatious joke or ignore the comment all together.

"Look, Mike—"

"Don't worry. I'm not going to tell your buddy what happened. Your secret's safe."

Conflicting feelings waged a war inside his body. Half of him burned hot from the scent of Michael's cologne, and the other half was as cold as ice from the shock of being alone with him, three feet from his parents' bed.

If Jared didn't get control of the defiant urge that had gripped him since the moment he had laid eyes on the ice cream bin at the gas station, he was likely to really do something insane, like fuck the hell out of Michael Crest before the end of the week.

The thought made his cock tingle. "I, uh, listen—"

"Jared. Breathe." Michael stepped closer. "I'm not gonna fuck anything up for you. What happened, happened, and I'm cool with it."

Jared exhaled.

Michael's brown eyes flickered even in the low lighting of the bedroom, and Jared recalled how Michael's warm mouth had wrapped around his cock. The thought of it made him horny as hell.

"I need to get my bag from the living room. Feel free to change in my parents' bathroom if you need to." He stalked toward the door and paused as he reached Michael. "I hope your ribs are okay." His gaze remained fixed on the floor, unable to look the other man in the eye.

Michael put his hand on Jared's shoulder. "Bruised, but not broken."

Jared nodded and left Michael alone in the bedroom. As he made his way back to the living room, he wondered if the "*bruised, but not broken*" comment had a double meaning. Had he hurt Michael with his behavior?

He wouldn't be surprised if he had. After all, if a girl had given him head in the woods out of the blue, Jared would be a dick for sure to ignore her afterward.

"Help yourselves to the beer and snack stuff, guys," he said.

"I'm gonna change into my swim suit," April said, taking Raul by the hand. "Wanna help?"

"Hot damn." Raul panted after her with his tongue wagging.

Jared turned back to Joel. "Glad y'all made it."

Joel grinned. "I didn't realize when we came that this was *your* place."

Jared glared hard at him. "*My* place?"

"Well, I've seen you around base, and Michael told me you helped him back to the infirmary when he fell this morning."

Jared's mind whirled. What else had Michael told his roommate? "Right. I thought that was him. I'm glad to see he's okay."

"Yep. He's fine."

Deep blue eyes glowered back at Jared as though daggers would fly out at any moment. Did Joel know?

"Michael's my best friend, and it's nice to know someone had his back out there."

"I was in the right place at the right time, I guess."

"Yeah, I guess you were."

"Well, I need to change, and then we can grab a cooler of beers and head down to the lake. How does that sound?"

"Sounds great to me," Alana said as she sauntered back into the living room.

"Okay, well you two get settled, and then we'll start this party." Jared grabbed his duffel bag and returned to his parents' bedroom.

As he entered, he noticed the bathroom door ajar

and saw Michael standing on the other side, pulling his shirt up over his head. White tape wrapped around his upper torso on one side, and Michael winced as he unfastened his jeans.

His ribs were definitely bruised.

Jared swallowed hard, standing there, watching, unable to look away. No matter how badly he wanted to leave, his feet wouldn't budge.

Michael lowered his jeans and then his boxers, causing Jared's cock to throb. Michael was gorgeous, with tanned skin, a tapered waist and an ass that curved perfectly, firm and supple.

Jared couldn't help it. He rubbed his dick through his tightening jeans. He'd never seen anything so appealing.

When Michael turned around, his rather large cock dangled between his legs, and Jared instantly wondered what it would feel like hard and in his hand. His pubic area was well groomed and trimmed very neatly, and his thighs were muscular and strong.

"Fuck."

Michael looked up, and the two men made eye contact.

Jared squirmed and quickly removed his hand from his crotch. His face burned as hot as a bonfire. *Shit!* He turned to go, but as he made it to the door, Michael rushed from the bathroom then reached out and grabbed his arm.

"You don't have to go."

Jared jerked back and licked his lips. He struggled not to look down. If he did, he wasn't sure what would happen, but he was sure it wouldn't be good. "Mike, I-I should leave."

"Don't."

The desperation in Michael's tone tugged at his

heart.

Jared backed against the door and stared into Michael's eyes. "Please don't."

"Don't what?" Michael pressed his lips together and inched closer. "Don't make you admit that you're attracted to me?"

Jared shook his head as Michael leaned into him.

"Don't tell you that you're all I think about?"

Hot breath spilled over Jared's neck as Michael quickly invaded his personal space. A warm hand gently took his, and in seconds, Jared held Michael's cock in his hand.

Michael caressed the back of Jared's fingers, prompting him to stroke his shaft. "See, it's only flesh and blood, just like yours."

Jared held his breath and squeezed his eyes shut as the softness of Michael's dick began to take on a different shape by hardening in his hand. He felt powerful. Strong. To know the effect his touch had on Michael excited him in a way he'd never been thrilled before.

All on his own, Jared continued to stroke it.

Michael leaned in and began to kiss Jared's neck. Soft moans vibrated against the tender skin on his throat, encouraging Jared to stroke faster.

Clicking sounds echoed throughout the room as his hand became slippery by the juices spilling from Michael's cock. Jared didn't have to look down to know instinctively what was occurring. He'd jacked off thousands of times. He'd know that sound anywhere.

Michael flattened his hand on the door beside Jared's head, keeping his body far enough away so as not to interrupt the event. He ran his tongue up Jared's jaw-line and toward his lips, then plunged it deep inside Jared's mouth.

His taste was as sweet as it had been that morning, maybe even more so. "Fuck."

Michael kissed him again and then pulled back, panting hard in Jared's ear. "I'm gonna come."

Jared's heart pounded. He'd never pleasured a man to the point of explosion, and the feeling of complete and utter supremacy flooded over his whole body. He opened his eyes and looked down as Michael's swollen cock pulsed in his hand. The tip dripped with satiny, clear pre-cum. Excited, Jared's fist slid up and down even faster.

Michael sucked air through his teeth. "Fuck yes."

Jared licked his lips, savoring the way Michael reacted to his touch.

Michael moaned, and then all of a sudden, he came.

One sweet burst after another of hot milky fluid spurted onto Jared's fingers. In that instant, Jared felt like a god.

Michael kissed him again, and for the first time ever, Jared held him in his arms and returned the kiss fervently.

"I've never enjoyed that before," Jared said before his mind had time to stop him.

"Seems we've had a lot of firsts today." Michael stepped back and scanned the room. "Towels?"

"In the bathroom."

Still unable to move from the spot, Jared remained standing with his back against the door. He watched Michael walk into bathroom then heard the sound of running water. Michael then emerged with a damp washcloth in his hand and a towel wrapped around his waist. Without skipping a beat, he cleaned his cum off of Jared's hand then returned to the bathroom again.

A million thoughts scattered across Jared's mind.

Some were full of wonder and excitement, leaving him somehow feeling fulfilled, complete. Then the words Michael had said moments ago came to mind. "You said something about firsts. What did you mean by that?"

Michael entered the room in dark blue swim trunks and grinned. "Do you think I make a habit of giving sexy guys blowjobs in the woods for the hell of it?"

Finally, Jared's feet separated from the floor, and he walked over to the bed and sat down. "Well, no, but I assumed you'd done it at some point."

Michael shook his head. "Not at all."

"Humph." Jared sat back, allowing the realization to sink in.

"I take it this wasn't your first time to jerk a guy off?"

"No, I mean yeah…Uh, not exactly."

Michael joined him on the bed. "Well which is it?"

"I did it when I was younger, but it definitely wasn't the same."

"You weren't feelin' it?'

Usually Jared avoided talking about his dark past, but for some reason his words flowed out like a fire hydrant spilling onto a neighborhood street whenever Michael was around. "No. It…it wasn't exactly my idea."

"Oh." Michael's tone changed from one of curiosity to perhaps understanding what Jared meant.

Jared silently nodded.

"I'm sorry if I pushed too hard then."

"No, I-I wanted to."

A wide grin spread across Michael's handsome face. "I know."

Jared stared into Michael's eyes. He did know. *Fuck!* How was that possible?

"Hey! Are you two losers going down to the lake with us or not?" Raul's voice carried down the hallway from the living room.

Jared sprang up, his heart pounding furiously in his chest. "God dammit! I forgot they were all here."

"It's okay, Jared. They're too preoccupied with the girls to worry about what we're doing. Besides, Joel and Alana will run interference."

"Joel and Alana know?"

"Joel's my roommate. There isn't much I can hide from him."

"Shit." Nausea bubbled up in his stomach. He certainly didn't need everyone knowing what happened in the woods that morning or what he'd just done to Michael.

"Seriously, Jared. It's okay to be gay in the military these days."

"Are you fucking serious? You think I'm gay?"

Michael stood. "Gay, bi, what difference does it make? It's nobody's business but yours."

Jared clenched his jaw taut and glared at Michael. "Listen, kid, there's a couple of things you don't know about Uncle Sam and Army policies. Just because they're not gonna ask, doesn't mean they want you to tell."

"There's something you need to understand, Jared Prophet. Refusing to admit it, doesn't mean you aren't what you are."

Jared stepped closer. "I'm. Not. Gay," he growled through clenched teeth.

"Well you damn sure aren't straight either, or did I imagine sucking you off this morning or your hand wrapped around my cock five minutes ago?"

Jared's face flared with fuming heat. He grabbed Michael by the shoulders and shook him hard. "Shut the fuck up!"

Michael's eyes widened, and his chest bowed. "Or what?"

Searching Michael's eyes, shame overcame his emotions, and Jared promptly released him. What the hell was he doing? "I'm sorry. I only—"

"Forget it." Michael flung the towel over his shoulder. "Trust me, it was nothing." He opened the door then disappeared down the hall.

Jared collapsed onto the bed, a flurry of twisted thoughts swirling in his head. *What the fuck is wrong with me?*

Chapter Five

The hot evening sun baked against Michael's skin as he floated out across the lake on one of the inflatable rafts Joel and Raul had found in the boat shed near the pier. Jared had yet to emerge from the house, and explaining why wasn't exactly an option.

Joel had been Michael's friend and confidant for quite some time, so had it only been Joel and Alana, the three of them would have discussed what had happened; and the couple would have offered unsolicited, though well-meaning, advice.

Alana's input would have been based on emotion and sensitivity, whereas Joel would have lacked the finesse needed when dealing with matters of the heart. His answer to the problem would have been a simple, *"Forget him, and move on."*

No, in this situation, Michael was best left to his own devices. The fewer people involved the better. There was more at stake than his bruised ego. In fact, Jared's issues might not have anything to do with him at all.

"Hey, wanna beer?" Joel called out.

Michael stretched his hand over his brow to block the relentless sun from his eyes. "Sure."

Joel grabbed a beer from the cooler, waded out into the water until he could swim and then slowly made his way to Michael. "Here." Joel tossed Michael the can.

"Thanks." Michael tapped the top a few times then popped it open. Cold foam poured over the side onto his hand. "It's hotter than hell out here."

"Good thing we have this lake, huh?"

"Yep."

Joel looked back at shore and Alana sat on her beach towel, cupping her hand over her eyes, exactly as Michael had done to block the sun. She watched them intently.

"Let me guess. You're on love connection duty."

Joel sighed. "If I don't help you out then she's gonna cut me off, dude."

Michael laughed. "No, she's not."

Joel's eyes widened. "I'm telling you, man, she said, and I quote, '*If Michael doesn't get any, neither do you*'."

"Well swim back over there and tell her not to worry."

Joel's mouth fell open. "Are you saying you hit that already?"

"Hit that?"

"You know, balls deep?"

Michael sat up and straddled the float. "Promise me you'll never use the words '*balls deep*' in my proximity again."

Joel's boisterous laugh carried across the lake. "Aw, man! You did, didn't you?"

Michael's face burned hot. "No, not yet, but something did happen."

"I don't need details." He held up his hand as if to deflect any information Michael might divulge.

"Good, because I wasn't giving you any." Michael leaned in closer and whispered, "Raul doesn't know anything about any of it, so make sure you don't say anything."

"Prophet's still in the closet?"

"So deep in the closet he can't even find himself."

"That's fucked up. I can't imagine that."

"Well, you're straight, so you don't have to hide anything from the world."

"He shouldn't have to either."

Michael couldn't agree more. "Not everybody has the support I've had. He'll have to deal with this in his own way."

"So what about you?"

"What about me?"

"Are you supposed to sit around and wait for this guy to man up?"

Michael considered the question for a moment. "I can't explain it, but for some reason, I understand him."

Joel offered a nod in lieu of a reply.

"Go back and reassure Alana that all is well in Michael-ville."

"Okay, but if she doesn't believe me and I don't get sex tonight, I'm gonna kick your ass."

"Don't worry, if Alana doesn't give you any, I will."

"Ha! Funny." Joel shoved the raft and began to swim away. "As long as I get to do you, we may be able to arrange something."

"Shut up!" Michael splashed him as Joel cackled another playful laugh.

"I'm just sayin'. Ass is ass in the dark."

"There are so many things wrong with you, I don't know where to begin," Michael called out as the distance between them widened.

He lay back on the float and savored the sun, periodically splashing water up onto his chest and legs to cool the slight burn. As he drifted toward the middle of the lake, Jared's voice bounced off the water, and Michael naturally looked toward shore.

Jared had emerged and stood between the two couples sunbathing on the bank. He wore red swim trunks and a white wife-beater tank so pristine the sun reflected off of it as though it were a lighthouse beacon. In seconds, he peeled it off, and for the first time, Michael got a good look at the rest of his physique.

His arms were as bulky as Michael had guessed,

and the ripples in his abs were noticeable even from across the lake. Michael barely made out the shape of what appeared to be a tattoo on his upper right bicep, and he immediately wondered what it was.

Jared stood tall and proud as he talked to the other four, and then Jared's attention turned toward Michael out in the water.

Michael's stomach fluttered with excitement at the thought of Jared looking his way.

Jared spread a towel off to the side, and stretched out along with everyone else.

Now Michael had no choice. He had to get closer.

Slowly paddling, he turned the raft around and forced it to float back toward shore. He had to be closer to Jared, even if the guy ignored him.

By the time he was only ten yards or so away, he heard their conversation much better.

"I think you two should go," Alana's voice echoed.

"Instead of having a pissing contest, you can have a midnight fishing competition." April's comment was next.

"Shit, it's too hot to fish during the day, so why not?" Raul chimed in.

"Okay. Well we only have one boat, so who wants it?" Jared asked.

Joel sat up and looked out at Michael. "Arrozo and I will take the boat. You and Crest fish from shore. The girls can chill in the house and do their nails."

The sound of the slap Alana gave to Joel's arm clattered across the water. "Ouch."

"You boys catch 'em and clean 'em, and April and I will cook 'em."

"Deal," Joel said.

Raul looked up at Michael. "That cool with you,

Crest?"

Michael avoided Jared's gaze and nodded. "Sure."

"Okay, well let's get this show on the road." Raul jumped up, and his stomach jiggled as he bent over to pick up his beer.

"Do either of you need a life vest?" Jared asked.

"Do I look like some kind of fairy to you?"

"No, you look like an overweight *borracho* who needs to do some sit-ups," Jared said.

"Fuck sit-ups, *ese*. But give me a few more beers, and I will definitely be a *borracho* tonight."

"Hey, don't think for one second I'm getting in that lake with your drunken ass rocking the boat. I can swim, but I'm not hauling you back to shore," Joel said.

"This *mojado* can swim under any circumstances." Jared laughed.

"Very funny and I'm not a wetback."

April got to her feet then jumped up onto Raul, wrapping her petite body around him. "You're so sexy when you're tough, *Papi*." She kissed him hard.

"Am I your sexy Mexican, *Mami*?" His voice raised an octave as the baby talk began.

"Damn straight." She winked.

A flurry of laughter broke out from the group.

Michael slipped off the raft and dragged it to shore. "Where are the poles?"

Jared glanced over at him then quickly looked away. "Over in the boat shed." He pointed toward the small building where Joel had found the rafts.

Joel shot up. "I'll show you."

Michael walked past Jared and followed Joel to the small building.

When they stepped inside Joel reached for a cluster of fishing poles leaning against the far wall. "I'll keep Raul busy, and Alana will contend with April. You and Prophet will pretty much have the place to yourselves tonight."

"I don't know if that's such a good idea, man."

"Michael, I saw the way he looked at you. Dude, you're in like Flynn." Joel shuddered as though repulsed. "Thank God, I don't have to fuck you now."

Michael laughed. "Like I'd even let you."

"What? Are you saying I'm not fuckable?"

"Not even in the same league as Jared Prophet."

"Damn. I can't even score with a dude. I'm losing my touch."

Michael patted his friend on the back. "My friend, I don't think you ever had it."

Joel grinned. "Probably not."

****

The moon rose fast, and the silence between Jared and Michael grew heavier by the minute until Michael couldn't take it anymore. "Are there even fish in this lake?"

They sat on the pier, their legs dangling over the side as they fished a few feet from one another.

Jared glanced over at him. "There used to be when I was a kid."

A wave of relief washed over Michael when Jared actually answered him. "Did your family come here a lot?"

"Pretty much every summer. My aunt and uncle brought their kids, too, and we'd turn it into a big family event."

"Sounds like you have a lot of great memories here."

"A few."

Michael sighed. "So, are you up for another beer?"

"Sure."

He stood, walked over to the cooler and dug out two beers from the slowlymelting ice, then handed one to Jared. "I hope we catch some fish. I haven't had anything other than beer all day."

"There's sandwich stuff in the house, if you're hungry."

Michael stared out at the moonbeams dancing on the water. "Nah, I'm good."

The silence quickly returned.

He glanced down and spotted a white rock jammed between the cracks of the pier. Michael squatted by the cooler, pulled it out and slung it sideways into the water hoping it would skip. "Ouch," he winced as a sharp pain sliced through his side.

"Those ribs will take a few days to heal."

"Yeah, in the meantime the beer will help to dull the pain."

"I have rum in the house if you want some."

"Maybe later." Michael exhaled hard, hoping to relieve the pressure. Would talking to Jared always be this strained? His nerves were already on edge from sitting so close. All he wanted to do was reach out and touch him.

Michael scanned the water and bank. The other guys were across the lake, too far to see clearly. A small lantern glowed in the distance from the bow of the boat.

Soft music echoed from inside the house. The girls were probably listening to CDs or watching TV.

"I think I'm gonna take a walk." He rose again and started back up the pier toward the bank. "Wanna come?"

Jared cocked his head to the side then laid his fishing pole down on the pier. "Sure. The fish damn sure aren't biting."

They strolled through the grass behind the house.

"It's peaceful here."

"Most of the time."

The slight rustle of leaves from a giant white oak tree resonated around them as a light breeze blew through the night.

"There's a trail over here that my cousin David and I made when we were probably around ten or so."

As they entered the woods, Michael followed close behind until the house completely disappeared from view. "That must have been cool. Of course, my friends and I would have built a fort if we'd had these woods all to ourselves."

Jared stopped and grinned so wide his white teeth flashed in the moonlight. "Oh, we did." His eyes brightened the dark night with an enthusiastic flare. "We had to keep it hidden from my dad, though. He would have bitched about it being a waste of time had he found it."

"Humph." Michael avoided further comment. He had a feeling he wouldn't care much for Jared's dad. Maybe that was one of the reasons Jared kept his true self hidden. Perhaps the fort was one of many secrets Jared felt the need to hide from his father. "You think the fort is still around?"

"It was the last time I was here. It's been a while though." Jared slowed and walked side by side with Michael.

Every once in a while their arms touched, and Michael tensed to prevent himself from grabbing Jared and kissing him.

Within a few moments, Jared stopped and turned toward Michael. "Okay. If I show you the fort, you have to swear not to tell a soul."

Michael chuckled and looked around. "Who am I going to tell? I don't even know where the hell I am."

A crooked grin broke across Jared's face as he stepped back and gestured to a dark cluster of broken tree branches and boards forming a lean-to between two crisscrossed pine trees that had fallen onto one another. "It's not the Ritz, but it was pretty badass back in the day."

Michael eased past him and squinted to get a better look in the dark. "It still looks pretty badass now." He pointed up to where the two trees met overhead. "X marks the spot."

When he turned, Jared stood right behind him, his chest mere inches from Michael's.

"I can't get you out of my fucking head," Jared whispered. His expression had hardened, and a sense of urgency bled through his serious tone.

"I know the feeling."

"What the hell am I supposed to do?"

Michael shook his head. "We figure it out."

Jared bit his bottom lip and shook his head. "That's just it. There is no figuring this shit out for me. I can't do it."

"Nobody says you have to do anything. This is your life, and you do what you need to do for you. But there's gonna come a day when you won't be able to hide it anymore, Jared. It'll eat at you from the inside out until you have no other choice. You either accept it, or you'll die inside."

"Death may be better." Jared's warm breath cascaded across Michael's face.

"You don't mean that."

"Don't I?"

"Don't say shit like that. There's always a way."

"Oh yeah?" Jared stepped closer. "Is there a way for me to leave you standing here without doing what I really want to do?"

"That depends?"

"On?"

"On what it is you want to do."

"If you were a girl, I'd have already fucked the shit out of you nine ways to Sunday."

Michael's stomach rippled with swirls of exhilaration. "And since I'm not?"

Without warning, the light in Jared's eye darkened, and a force, impossible to prepare for, slammed into him, knocking him back several feet.

Jared had shoved him. Hard.

Michael regained his footing and stood up straight. His heart pounded like a bass drum. "I won't ever be a girl, Jared."

"Fuck you."

"No. Fuck you."

Jared ran at him and clipped him at his waist.

A fire of pain shot across Michael's chest as he fell back onto the ground with Jared on top of him.

"God dammit! Why couldn't you leave me the fuck alone?"

"I'm not the problem," Michael growled as he struggled to breath with Jared's weight bearing down on his chest.

Jared grabbed Michael's head and squeezed.

The pressure was almost unbearable. "Go ahead," Michael shouted, fighting back tears. "Kill me!"

Veins jutted out on Jared's neck and forehead and his face turned beet red. "God damn you!" He released Michael's head, and in a flash, he kissed him hard, shoving his tongue deep into Michael's mouth.

Michael opened his eyes to see tears streaming down Jared's cheeks. He cupped Jared's face and wiped them away with his thumbs. "I'm here. It's okay. You don't have to hide from me."

"I don't know what to do." Jared cried.

"We don't have to figure it out right now. There's no hurry, trust me."

Jared kissed him again then rolled over onto his back.

Michael coughed to relieve the tightness still constricting his ribcage. He drew in a couple of deep breathes, then sat up and lingered over the other man. Michael pressed his hand against Jared's chest. "Look at me."

Jared's head turned in his direction, and red, puffy eyes glared back at him.

"This is new for me, too. I've never felt this way about anyone. All I know is that what you do to me is right."

Jared shook his head as if prepared to argue.

Michael put his finger across Jared's lips. "Don't talk. Don't argue. Don't do anything except what *feels* right."

Jared reached out for Michael and ran his fingers through his hair. "*You* feel right."

"Then we start there."

Sitting up, Jared looked around the woods. "We destroyed my fort."

Michael dusted the dirt off of Jared's back. "Fuck it. We'll build a better one."

Smiling eyes found Michael in the dark. "When we get back to the house, after everyone goes to bed, I want you to come to my room." He stood and began to clean the dirt and leaves off of himself.

"Why? So you can beat the shit out of me?" Michael got to his feet and did the same.

"I'm sorry. I don't know why I get so pissed. Fighting seems to be the only way I know how to deal with what's going on in my head." He glared down at the ground between them. "I promise I only want to talk."

"It's okay. I can handle a little aggression, but don't push it." Michael offered a slight smile.

Jared flicked a broken twig out of Michael's hair and skimmed over his cheek with a gentle touch that Michael instinctively leaned in to. With a subtle tug, Jared pulled Michael closer.

Michael gazed deeply into Jared's eyes, and a sense of tenderness blanketed the air. Jared drew in a deep breath then kissed him.

After a few seconds, Jared broke away and pressed his forehead against Michael's. "You're gonna be the end of me, kid."

Michael narrowed his gaze, trying his best not to be angry at the innocent comment and looked him square in the eyes. "I'm no kid, Prophet."

Jared chuckled and sighed. "No. You're definitely not."

Chapter Six

"Where the hell have you two been?" Raul asked as they walked into the house.

"I wanted to show Crest where my uncle shot a bobcat when I was fourteen, but the dumbass tripped over a tree stump and nearly broke both our necks," Jared lied.

He glanced over at Michael, hoping he'd go along with the cover story he'd mentally concocted as they walked back to the house.

"Bobcat?" April asked with wide eyes. "Seriously?"

"Don't worry, if there are any dangerous animals out there, Michael damn sure scared them off," Jared said.

"Well if I had something more than fucking beer in my stomach today, I may have been sober enough to see through the briar patch you dragged me through."

Alana jumped to her feet. "Want me to make you a sandwich, Mikey?"

"Hey, I asked you to make me a sandwich earlier and you flipped me off." Joel folded his arms across his chest.

Alana's fingers playfully tiptoed across Michael's chest. She clutched his shirt collar and brought his head down to meet her face then gave him a quick peck on the lips.

The hair on the nape of Jared's neck stood on end at the thought of anyone other than him touching Michael.

"Well, you're not Michael." Alana pranced in a full circle around Michael then wrapped her arms around his waist. She looked up at Michael and winked. She then draped herself around his neck, practically hanging from him as though he were a human jungle gym.

What's up with that? Jared glared at the two of them standing in the middle of the room, looking more like lovers than friends. He cleared his throat. "There should be enough in there for a few sandwiches. If you're too busy with your roommate's girlfriend, *Mikey,* I'd be happy to make enough for all of us."

"Oh, no you don't." Alana slurred her words, obviously drunker than Jared first thought. "I'm gonna take care of Mikey tonight." She patted his cheek then squeezed. "Look at this face. He's so cute with these sexy little dimples."

"Okay, that's enough." Joel got to his feet. "You're so drunk you'll probably get lost before you make it into the kitchen. I'm taking you to bed."

"Bed?" She giggled. "Are you gonna get lucky tonight?" Her voice dropped to a low, but playful tone.

Joel scooped her up under her armpits and detached her from Michael's neck. "You tell me. Am I gonna get lucky tonight?" He started to drag her down the hall toward the room Jared had given them.

Alana struggled and tried to pull away, seemingly more content to focus her attention on Michael. "I don't know. Let's ask Mikey." She snorted a laugh. "Hey, Mikey!" Her laughter increased. "I've always wanted to say that. Get it? Hey, Mikey? Like the cereal commercial?"

"Yeah, I get it." Considering Joel's scowl, he wasn't as amused as she appeared to be.

"Hey, Mikey?" She used the playful tone once again.

"Yes, Alana?"

"Is Joel gonna get lucky tonight?"

A brief flutter of excitement dashed across Jared's insides as Michael cast an uneasy glance at him then returned his attention to Alana. "Yes, Alana, Joel's getting very lucky tonight."

She laughed aloud followed by a rather harsh hiccup. "I knew it." Her body instantly went limp, and her head slumped over onto Joel's shoulder. She was out.

"Looks like *Joel* won't be getting as lucky he'd hoped," Joel picked her up and cradled her in his arms. "Thanks a lot, *Mikey*. Good night, everybody."

Several "*good nights*" reverberated around the room as Joel carried Alana down the hall to their bedroom.

Jared glanced over at Raul and April who had snuggled on the sofa and had begun to make out rather passionately. "Hey, get a room." *Why don't they go to bed already? Damn!*

Michael sauntered over and sat on the opposite end of the couch. "Unless of course this is gonna become a threesome, considering you're making out in my bed."

"Ooh." April winked. "Sounds fun, *Mikey*."

"Fuck that!" Raul said. "If there's gonna be a threesome in my future, it'll be with two chicks."

April slipped up onto his lap and straddled him. "That might work, too." She giggled.

Jared shook his head. He could care less about threesomes. All he wanted was to have Michael all to himself before the feeling of euphoria wore off completely, and he came back to his senses.

"Well, I'm gonna make a stack of sandwiches for myself and go to my room. You three have fun."

Michael stretched his legs out under the coffee table in front of the sofa and rested his head on the back. He peered over at him and smiled a crooked smile.

Jared's stomach fluttered. So much had changed in the last twenty-four hours. He looked up at the clock above the kitchen table. *Zero three hundred already?* As late as it was, he'd never get to spend any time with

Michael before daylight.

He rushed around the kitchen and made four very thick sandwiches. Two for him and two for Michael. Then he grabbed two cold beers from the refrigerator, and headed for the bedroom.

As he passed through, Michael appeared to have fallen asleep, and Raul and April were still kissing pretty hot and heavy on the sofa beside him.

Shit! "Raul," he said as he nudged his foot. "I think Crest may want to go to bed."

Raul and April separated and looked up at him.

Jared gestured to a sleeping Michael beside them.

"A'ight, man. We'll go to bed in a second."

Jared shook his head, frustrated, but decided it would be best not to make big deal about it. Further comment would only draw unwanted curiosity as to why he cared if Michael got any sleep or not.

He went to his room, put the plate of sandwiches on the nightstand and set the two beers next to it.

"Shit," he cursed under his breath. "I smell like spoiled lake water." He sniffed his shirt and pulled it over his head as he rushed into the bathroom.

Jared shucked off his swim trunks and turned on the water to the shower. Steam immediately filled the room.

He checked under the sink cabinet and brought out a bottle of shampoo and a new bar of soap. His mother always brought extras every time they came so they would be sure never to run out. She was a great planner in that respect.

He hopped into the shower and applied shampoo to his hair. If he'd had time, he'd have grabbed a razor, but he hadn't thought of it. All he cared about was getting the smell of the lake off of his body, not to mention the dirt and muck from his tussle in the woods with Michael.

He lathered his body with soap and was about to rinse, when he turned to find Michael standing outside the bathtub, naked.

"Room for two?"

Jared swallowed hard, and his cock pulsated as blood rushed to meet his growing need. He said nothing and inched back.

Michael came to him and ran a gentle touch across his chest. "I've waited so long to see you like this."

Jared eyed Michael up and down. Water cascaded off of his chest, and his tanned skin glistened.

"You had your fill of me earlier this afternoon, now I get to look at you."

Jared held his breath as Michael gave him the once over. He slid slippery fingers over the tattoo on his upper right arm, and Jared tried to imagine what Michael thought of the twin snakes twisted around a dagger inked over a traditional red cross. He'd chosen a tattoo to signify his loyalty to God, Country and the unity of combat medics.

His stomach swirled as Michael's hand trailed across his flesh. "You're so sexy."

Jared inhaled deep as gooseflesh riddled his body. "Fuck." He tried to remain calm. His dick throbbed, on the verge of eruption at the mere thought of Michael touching him.

Michael grabbed the bar of soap from the dish mounted on the wall and handed it to Jared. "Don't be shy."

Jared squeezed the bar as Michael turned and faced away from him. The man's athletic physique was amazing.

He glided the soap across Michael's shoulders and down the middle of his back. His hand trembled as he slid it over Michael's ass.

Michael's muscles flexed, and deep indentions sank into his ass cheeks.

Jared had to go there. He *needed* to go there.

Suds saturated his hand, and before he knew it he had ventured between Michael's cheeks. The bar slipped down between their feet and only Jared's soapy fingers remained.

Soft tissue tightened around Jared's index finger, and Michael moaned, causing Jared's cock to flinch.

Michael backed up forcing Jared's finger to press into him deeper.

Jared stopped, and his heart boomed so loud it was all he heard. The slick entrance of Michael's hole was soft. He felt every bump where it gathered to form a tight seal over the hole. His cock brushed against the back of Michael's thigh, and hair pricked the sensitive tip, not uncomfortably, but enough to tickle.

Michael leaned back, pressing his back to Jared's chest. "I trust you," he said breathlessly, breaking through the trance-like feeling that had engulfed Jared's mind.

Curiosity prevailed, and Jared ran his left hand around Michael's side and hugged him close, while trailing across his shoulder with his tongue. His index finger passed the point of no return and sank farther into Michael's ass.

Michael tensed, and Jared's finger became wedged within tight spongy walls. "Relax," Jared whispered into his ear.

The muscles released him, and Jared continued inside, deeper, then slowly back out until only the tip of his finger remained. He dropped to his knees, spread Michael's cheeks apart with his left hand and watched his finger delve inside again. It disappeared past the knuckle, and warm, slick tissue swallowed his finger, almost sucking it in all on its own. He eased it out and added another digit to his endeavor, then carefully plunged back in.

Michael squirmed. He bent over slightly, holding his palms flat against the shower wall, causing water to flood over Jared's hand.

Jared was committed now. He had to test the limits as his cock pulsated and his balls hung heavier than they ever had. His mouth watered, and he leaned in and kissed Michael's ass. Soon his tongue lapped the waterfall trickling between his cheeks, and Michael groaned even louder.

Jared dared to venture even further. He had no idea what he was supposed to do, but it wasn't rocket science. He'd done this to Tiffany many times. He was quite a bit more in to it now, and his main concern was to impress, not to simply go through the motions as he had done with her.

Jared then twisted his wrist, causing his fingers to curl upward inside Michael's ass.

And that's when it happened.

The tip of his finger grazed a rigid object about two inches in, and Michael practically climbed the walls, writhing onto Jared's hand. "Fuck, fuck, oh, fuck!"

Exhilarated, Jared flicked it again.

Michael reached back, grabbed Jared's hand and shoved him in deeper.

All bets were off. Jared had found Michael's spot.

Michael gripped his cock with his other hand and began to stoke his own shaft. While Jared continued to assault his ass with tender kisses mixed with a few nibbles, he worked his fingers in and out until he heard the words he'd longed to hear. Words he'd waited his whole life to hear, but never knew he wanted to.

"I need you inside me."

Jared stood, his cock pulsing relentlessly. "Are you sure?"

Michael nodded enthusiastically, water drenching his chiseled face.

"Not without a condom."

Michael turned and faced him. "This is my first time. It's okay."

Jared looked him in the eyes, and for the first time in his life, shame and disappointment overwhelmed his heart. He lowered his head. "But it's not my first time."

Michael lifted Jared's chin, forcing eye contact. "It's okay. I understand."

But it wasn't okay. Not for Jared. "I don't want to take any chances with you. Some of the women I've been with—"

"None of that matters." Michael shut off the water and took Jared by the hand. He led him from the shower to the bed and sat down, soaking wet. "I know you have condoms around here somewhere." His dick flopped onto his leg, semi-hard, and it took all the strength Jared had not to reach for it and stroke it as he had done earlier in the day. He longed for that feeling of power.

Instead, Jared smiled and went to his duffel bag on the floor against the wall across from the bed. He retrieved the condoms he'd brought in the event Raul had actually brought the girls he'd promised.

Michael laughed. "Always prepared like a Boy Scout."

"I was never a Boy Scout."

"Good." He took the condoms from Jared's hand. "Then you won't be able to get loose if I decide to tie you up."

Jared's heart fluttered. "Tie me up?" He'd never even contemplated such a thing, but suddenly, the possibility of things he'd never done before seemed endless.

Michael chuckled. "You're so easy to excite. Go lock the door while I open this pack."

Jared did as he was told for no other reason than to please Michael. This had unexpectedly become his top priority. Whatever Michael Crest wanted, he'd damn sure give him. No questions asked.

He returned to Michael and stood before him. Jared's cock was hard as a rock and stood at attention, undeterred by the distractions and delay. Michael had a way of making him hard in an instant and kept him that way much longer than Jared had ever experienced.

The condom was cold to the touch, and Jared jolted as Michael slid it down his shaft. He looked up at him, and Jared felt an uncontrollable urge to pull him close and hold him. He thought better of it though. That's how you treated a girl. Men didn't like that cuddly bullshit.

Michael crawled up on the bed and crooked his finger at Jared inviting him to join him. Jared didn't hesitate. He needed to feel Michael close. Jared didn't care whether men were supposed to like it or not.

Michael's body was warm, and Jared rubbed his chest, paying close attention to his tiny erect nipples. They fascinated him. How strange it was not to have plump breasts and larger buds to lick and suck. He'd always fancied himself a breast man. He'd been wrong.

Jared lapped at Michael's nipples, and curiosity weighed heavily. How would his dick taste? He'd had oral sex with women and admittedly enjoyed pleasuring them, but this was different. This was something he had an innate feeling about. He knew how he liked to have his dick sucked. Well at least he had thought he did until Michael gave him head. That level of pleasure was new, as well.

Jared moved down Michael's body, kissing, licking, tasting every inch of him. When he felt Michael's cock touch his cheek, Michael laughed.

"You need to shave."

Jared rubbed his jaw and felt the stubble that had grown out since morning. A sadistic urge overtook him, and he immediately scraped his cheek across Michael's dick again. Pubic hair tickled back. "How about we shave everything tomorrow? And I do mean *everything*." He grinned.

Michael's Adam's apple bobbed up and down. "Are you sure you want to do this?"

"Do what?"

"What you're about to do."

Jared's needs changed as a desire to tease rushed to the surface. "What am I about to do?" His own confidence astounded him. Had he always been this assertive? He tried to recall, but it was as if every experience he'd ever had in his life swiftly faded away into little more than a faint memory. Even Tiffany had been banished from his mind.

"I think you were about to suck my—" Michael gasped and shoved his head back into the pillow when Jared's tongue flicked the tip of his cock.

He licked down the shaft and back again, amused by Michael's reaction. Slipping him into his mouth, Jared relaxed his jaw to accommodate more of the shaft. It was easier than he'd imagined.

Michael gripped the base and held himself still while Jared continued the up and down motion of sucking him off, breaking his rhythm only to lick and slurp the pre-cum drizzling from the tip. After a few moments, Jared remembered why they had come to the bed to begin with when his own cock began to pulsate with need.

He sucked Michael's balls and gently lifted them with his fingertip revealing the taint. Jared slowly flattened his tongue against the perineum between Michael's ballsack and ass then probed it several times.

Michael squirmed.

Jared moved down and teased Michael by tonguing his hole once again. He spat on his index finger then massaged the area he'd conquered in the shower. It all came back to him, where Michael's spot was and how he'd reacted when Jared found it. Jared rushed to get Michael back to that place again.

One finger in, then two, and Michael was putty in his hands.

Michael moaned and sucked air in through his teeth. His body tensed with each and every swipe of his prostate. He drew his knees up to his chest, allowing Jared full access to his ass. "God damn. Are you sure you've never done this before?"

Jared paused. "Not like this." He enthusiastically returned to his mission.

Michael jacked off, his fingers tapping Jared's forehead with each quickening stroke.

"Don't come," Jared said. "I want to see it when you do, and I'm not done yet."

"Shit." Michael panted. He released his cock and twisted the sheets around his fists. "You've teased me enough."

Michael was right. They had both been tortured long enough. "I need lubricant. You're too dry."

"In my bag." Michael gestured to his duffel bag on the floor next to Jared's.

Jared bolted from the bed, unzipped the bag and dumped everything onto the floor. The small tube of cinnamon-flavored lube landed on top. "Cinnamon?"

"My mind was set on having you one way or the

other. I came prepared."

"Now who's the fucking Boy Scout?" Jared grinned. He slid into the bed and stretched out down the length of Michael's body.

Michael turned on his side, facing away.

Jared squeezed the contents of the lube onto his fingers and massaged Michael's asshole, dipping his finger inside a couple of times to make sure he was well lubed.

He then secured the condom and guided his cock between Michael's ass cheeks and held his breath. Kissing the back of Michael's neck, he whispered, "Relax, baby." Natural affection came so easily.

Michael's body reacted instantly, and Jared slowly applied pressure to Michael's hole and entered. Jared ventured in, then pulled out several times until the sphincter muscle relaxed and accommodated the head.

After a few more tries, Michael moaned, reached back and grasped Jared's thigh, drawing his cock deeper inside.

Jared lay there, allowing Michael to rock his hips back and forth on his shaft until every throbbing inch of Jared's cock had been consumed by Michael's ass.

Heaven.

Jared could hardly contain his emotions as his need to come grew. Taking Michael by the hand, he silently encouraged him to stroke himself, and Jared then returned to his original intent.

He eased in and out, keeping pace with Michael's groans and labored pants. Their bodies had merged naturally and acted as one entity, blowing any thought of ever being an individual again completely out of Jared's mind. Michael was his, and nothing would change that.

"Jared?" Michael whispered in the glow of predawn light seeping through the bedroom window.

"Hmm?" He pounded into him feverishly. His balls slapped back and forth between Michael's ass, his thighs and the bed.

"Don't fucking stop."

"I couldn't if I tried." He kissed Michael's neck and held him close, puffing into his ear. "Fuck, I'm coming." A surge the size of what felt like a tidal wave erupted from his cock, and Michael's ass instantly clenched taut around him, nearly taking his breath away.

Jared's body twitched in ecstasy as a monstrous orgasm damn near destroyed what was left of his already reeling mind.

"Watch." Jared heard the words and struggled to pry his eyes open. As he did, milky white semen spewed from Michael's cock and splattered onto the bed in front of them. Another blast followed, and then another.

Chills skittered across Jared's stomach, and Michael turned and faced him. Sweat dripped from his hair, and his eyes sparkled like melted, creamy chocolate. His cheeks and throat were tinted dark red, and gooseflesh riddled his golden skin.

Jared ran his hand down the length of Michael's arm then came to rest on his hip. "Are you okay?"

Michael nodded, but didn't speak.

"I hope I did it right."

Michael closed his eyes and moved in for a kiss. "That was perfect."

Jared kissed him back.

A cool breeze blew across their wet bodies as the air conditioner kicked on.

Jared reached down to the bottom of the bed and pulled the blankets up over them as Michael nuzzled under his chin.

In a matter of minutes, both fell asleep.

TYLER ROBBINS

Chapter Seven

Michael woke to find Jared sprawled across the bed, naked and looking like he'd run a marathon. The sheets were still damp, and a used condom lay between them.

Michael's heart quivered as he recalled making love to Jared most of the night. Hell, they'd started early in the morning the day before back at the base, picked up again in the afternoon, then finished it off with mind-blowing sex all night.

He shook his head in disbelief. Had he dreamt it?

As he sat up, pain shot through his body, this time not from his bruised ribs, but from his throbbing ass. "Shit." The burn grew more intense.

Easing out of the bed, so as not to wake Jared, Michael carefully made his way to the bathroom. He stood in front of the toilet and tried to urinate. No such luck.

His ass pulsed, and he thought he'd never be able to sit down again. Surely it wouldn't always be that way. He glanced back over to the bed where Jared lay sleeping. Drawing in a deep breath, he smiled. The discomfort didn't matter. It was all worth it.

He splashed water on his face and studied his reflection in the mirror. He didn't look any different, but he damn sure felt different. Not because his ass throbbed, but because of the way his skin tingled as memories of Jared's mouth on his skin rushed through his mind. Jared's touch, his kisses, his inquisitive exploration of places neither had been and their shared experiences far surpassed anything Michael had ever imagined.

As far as first *"everythings"* went, Jared Prophet had handled them all with the precision of a master craftsman. Jared was a wonderful lover, and Michael couldn't wait to return the favor.

He bit his bottom lip, continuing to watch Jared sleep. Every inch of the man glistened in the morning light.

Michael glanced down at his watch. "Damn." Morning was almost over.

He gathered his clothes, dressed quickly and opened the bedroom door as quietly as possible. He hoped everyone was still asleep. Well, he hoped Raul and April were. It really didn't matter if Joel and Alana were or not. He had no secrets where they were concerned.

He tiptoed down the hall and nearly jumped out of his skin when Joel ran smack into him as he rounded the corner to the kitchen.

"Well, look at you. That's a walk of shame of I ever saw one."

"Shhh," Michael whispered.

"Screw them."

Michael shook his head. "Seriously, man. This has to stay between the four of us."

"Uh uh." Joel's brow jutted upward. "Leave me out of it. If you feel the need to share, talk to your little girly-friend. She's about to drive me crazy with anticipation."

"Girly-friend?"

"Yeah. I figure she has you for the girly stuff and me for the…" He thumbed the side of his nose like a boxer preparing for a fight, adopting an air of masculine swagger. "*Manly stuff.*" His voice dropped so deep, he sounded like he'd overdosed on steroids.

"You're such an asshole, you know that?" Michael walked past him and opened the refrigerator door. Beer lined the shelves. He grabbed one, popped it open and gulped down a few swallows, then belched rather loudly. "I'm manly, too."

Joel slapped him on the back. "Okay, so you're manly, too."

Michael went into the living room and eased down onto the sofa, careful not to move too fast. "I know what you mean though. You don't want to discuss sex with me."

"Oh, we can discuss sex all day of it involves tits and ass."

Michael cast a devious grin in his direction. "I can do half of that."

Joel grimaced and feigned a heart attack, nearly collapsing to his knees as he approached the sofa. "Let me rephrase that. Tits and pussy."

Michael laughed, "Sorry, man, you'll have to rely on Raul for that."

Joel plopped down on the couch beside him, sending electrifying jolts of pain up into Michael's stomach. Unable to help himself, he winced.

"Damn, bro. I'm sorry. I forgot about your ribs."

Michael tried to catch his breath and wagged his finger at Joel to correct him. "Not the ribs, dude."

Joel's mouth dropped open. He'd obviously picked up on what Michael meant and followed up with an animated groan. "That's gotta suck."

Michael eased back and rested his head on the sofa, trying his best not to move. "You have no idea."

"Man, all I can say is I hope it was worth it."

Heat rushed to Michael's face. He glanced over at his best friend and repeated the same words, "*You have no idea.*" Though now they took on a totally different meaning.

Both laughed until once again, Joel shuddered and shook his head. "Dude, seriously though, I'm happy for you."

Joel was happy for him, and Michael knew that. They had discussed the subject at great length when they first became roommates. Michael had been honest with him and told him right away he didn't have to worry about Michael becoming attracted to him. As far as Michael was concerned, straight guys were immediately off limits, and in return Joel had assured Michael, if at any time he became uncomfortable, he'd tell him and they'd work it out like adults.

As it turned out, Joel's Uncle was gay, so he'd been raised understanding that people are who they are and there was no way to change it. Michael had lucked out having Joel as a roommate and friend.

Joel had a great sense of humor about it, too, and promised that if Michael ever turned *him* on, Michael would be the first to know. Then he went on to add that in the event he ever had a monster case of blue balls he wasn't above asking Michael for a blow job as long as they kept it between them. They joked that what happened in their apartment stayed in their apartment.

"Where's Alana?"

"She and April drove up to the store for donuts and coffee. I guess the ladies can't handle beer in the morning."

"Not like us *manly* men," Michael said.

"Raul's out fishing. Can't keep that Mexican out of the boat."

"Did y'all catch anything last night?"

"Mosquitoes the size of Alaska."

Michael laughed. "Yeah, they're getting bad."

"Probably because the tropical storm is pushing them north." Joel got up and went to the kitchen. "I listened to the news this morning," he said. "They say it's right below hurricane force winds and should hit the coast later tonight."

Michael sat up straight. "Did they say where?"

"Anywhere between Port Arthur and Corpus Christie."

"Where?" Jared asked as he entered the room wearing an unbuttoned pair of jeans and no shirt. Every muscle in his buff body screamed sex-god. He should seriously come with a warning sign hanging around his neck.

Michael's stomach whirled like a tornado had been unleashed inside him at first sight.

"Morning," Joel said. "The news said Tropical Storm Constance may be upgraded to a hurricane if the winds keep escalating and will hit pretty much anywhere along the coast."

"Damn. My family lives southeast of Houston. That puts them right in the middle of it."

This information had Michael's full attention. "Will they evacuate?" *And if so, will they come here?*

Jared shook his head. "No. My dad's one of those guys who would rather go down with his ship than admit defeat and run for the hills."

"Evacuating and running are two different things."

"Not according to Jonathan Prophet." Jared leaned against the wall. "I'll call my mom later and check on them."

"Wanna beer?" Joel called out with his head in the refrigerator.

"Nah, I was thinking to gather some wood and build a fire for tonight. We can roast marshmallows and cook those hot dogs."

"Good idea," Michael said.

Jared looked over at him, and his cheeks flared red. He licked his lips and flashed Michael a crooked, but sexy smile.

Michael's head spun with excitement. "I'll help." He scooted to the edge of the sofa, then closed his eyes and held his breath as the sharp sting shot through his lower abdomen again.

"You okay?" Deep lines creased Jared's forehead. He was concerned.

Joel entered the room. "He'll be okay. An anaconda bit him on the ass, so he won't be break dancing tonight. That's for sure."

Jared's eyes widened, and his neck and face turned ten shades of red.

"I'm fine." Michael gave Joel a dirty look. "Joel's pissed because he didn't get any last night, so you'll have to excuse his sour mood." He got up and walked past Joel, headed to the bedroom. "Do you mind if I use your bathroom?"

"No. Go right ahead."

"Well don't go slipping Alana any alcohol tonight. You both have a lot to make up for." Joel's voice carried down the hall, but Michael ignored him.

Michael showered, brushed his teeth and shaved. Nothing was going to ruin the day or his overwhelming sense of contentment.

As he emerged from the bathroom, he found Jared sitting on the bed. His expression immediately caught Michael's attention. "I was gonna change the sheets and found this." Jared held the sheet in his hand as he glared at the floor.

"What's wrong?" Michael moved closer.

"Did I hurt you?"

Michael swallowed hard. "No." What was he talking about?

"There's blood."

Michael looked down and saw the smear, most likely from the side where he had slept. "Jared, things got a little intense, but I'm good."

Jared stood and dropped the sheet. "How can you be good if I made you bleed?"

Michael cupped the right side of his face. "Think of it like a girl losing her cherry. You popped mine, and I lived to love another day." He chuckled and caressed Jared's cheek with his thumb.

"I'm glad you think this is so funny."

Michael kissed him. "Go take a long, hot shower. I'll be outside gathering wood for your bonfire."

"Are you sure?"

"Dude, let it go."

Jared nodded though his expression was far from agreeable. "Don't gather any wet stuff."

Michael spun around. "I *was* a Boy Scout, remember? I know how to start a fire."

Jared finally relented, and his lips stretched into a sincere smile as he entered the bathroom.
****

The day seemed to fly by. Michael spent most of the afternoon being debriefed by Alana. She followed him around like a curious child asking details so private Michael squirmed on more than one occasion. He finally told her that if she asked one more question, he'd never tell her anything again. It worked.

As they floated across the lake, Michael took advantage of his dark sunglasses and watched Jared build a fire. He tried not to drool, but every time Raul commented on a conversation with his chest-pounding, dick-swinging, knuckle-dragging view on life, Michael quickly remembered they were in mixed company.

He understood now what life was like for Jared. Michael wasn't naïve, nor did he see the world through rose-colored glasses. He had experienced derision from ignorant homophobes and had endured his share of insults and snide remarks, but he'd never really allowed those kinds of things to bother him, until now. Until now, he hadn't had anything to lose.

Jared was important, and his inability to deal with opponents of gays and lesbians was something Michael had to tread around lightly. He had to be careful not to push.

By the time the sun had gone down and everyone had gathered around the fire, he'd hardly said ten words to Jared, and it was killing him to intentionally avoid him. He'd chosen to keep his distance, so Jared would see he wasn't clingy and he wasn't going to invade his personal space.

What he really wanted to do was sit next to him and watch the fire, talk and maybe even fool around.

That wouldn't happen with Raul and April there. In fact, if Jared didn't get over his fear of people discovering who he was, it might never happen at all. It sucked being at the mercy of fear and ignorance.

The night became almost stagnant by the time they finished eating, and beer took on a totally different taste, no longer appealing to Michael. He needed something stronger. Hell, he needed to get shit-faced drunk, and then maybe the party would liven up.

Joel and Alana cuddled beside him, and Jared sat to his left, leaning against a log he'd rolled out from the woods.

Raul and April were spread out on a sleeping bag on the opposite side of the fire. The radio, tuned in to some country music station, faded in and out every few minutes or so. They turned it up at any mention of the tropical storm making landfall somewhere between Galveston and Port Arthur. It wouldn't reach their area, but they were definitely expecting some bad weather caused by Constance.

"Dance with me," Alana said to Joel.

"Me? Dance?" Joel shook his head and laughed. "What will I get if I do?"

Alana giggled and kissed him. "Won't know until you do." She stood up and reached for him to take her hand.

Joel got up and scooped her up into his arms, whirling her around and laughing.

Michael glanced over at April, who nudged Raul as though inviting him to dance with her.

Raul shook his head. "I'm not dancing."

"Fine, then." Her attention instantly snapped to Michael. "What do ya' say?"

Michael looked to Raul to make sure he didn't mind. He responded with a shrug, so Michael went over and took her by the hand. "I have two left feet, so watch your toes," he said.

"Well I have two right feet, so we should be fine." She grinned from ear to ear.

Michael slipped his arm around her waist and pulled her close. He hadn't danced with a girl since his senior prom. Though his memory of it was a bit of a blur, he'd had a great time.

"You're pretty good at this," April said.

Michael smiled and nodded. "I'm simply swaying to the music."

Her head barely came to the middle of his chest. She had to have been the tiniest girl he'd ever danced with.

He looked over her head at Jared who eyed them closely. He wasn't exactly smiling, but he wasn't frowning either. Michael couldn't read his mood. *Was he jealous or disinterested altogether?*

If things were different, he would be standing there in Jared's arms, but things were what they were.

April interrupted his thoughts. "So how old are you?"

"Almost twenty-one."

"Hmm." She seemed to ponder his reply.

His curiosity flared. "Why?"

"I'm curious as to why you're single. You're smart, sexy and very good looking. A real catch."

An uneasy pinch gathered in his stomach as though his insides were being bound into a knot. He slowed his movement, contemplating his answer. "I guess I'm not the settling type. I want what I want, and I won't take anything less."

"So you do have a type?"

"Oh yeah." Michael's mind conjured up images of Jared sprawled out naked in a bed. "I definitely have a type."

She tilted her head to the side. "Let me guess. Blonde?"

Her reply intrigued him, and for a split second, he wondered if she'd picked up on the vibes between him and Jared. He'd feel her out to be sure. "As a matter of fact, I do have a soft spot for blonds."

"Damn!" She snapped her fingers. "I was hoping you would say you were in to short, petite, brunettes."

Michael's cheeks warmed. No, she hadn't figured him out at all. Part of him was relieved. Jared's secret was still safe and sound. But at the same time, another part was sad there had to be secrets at all. "Are you kidding? Short, petite, brunettes are at the top of my list." He laughed. "That is if they're single and don't have a boyfriend who carries a club and hunts dinosaurs on his days off."

April laughed, too. "He is a bit of a Neanderthal, isn't he?"

"He's okay," Michael said. "Once you get past

those rough edges."

April laid her head on his chest and hugged him close.

A melancholy mood seemed to instantly shift over her. Why would she continue to date Raul if the truth about him made her so blue? He smoothed down the back of her hair, hoping to give her a little reassuring comfort.

April was a nice girl, and she didn't seem to be the kind who would tolerate a man with such chauvinistic ideals. Then again, who was Michael to judge? He knew very little about her. Looks were often-times deceiving. After all, if they weren't, everyone would know Jared's deep, dark secret.

"What the fuck do you think you're doing?" Raul's voice boomed from the other side of the fire where he stood with his hands planted firmly on his hips. His brow pinched with anger.

Michael stepped back and looked around.

Joel let go of Alana and held up his hand in front of Raul. "They're only dancing, man."

"Excuse me?" Michael asked as he separated himself from April. "What's your problem?"

"My problem is the asshole with the balls to make the moves on my girl right in front of me." Raul pushed past Joel.

"Raul! Stop it!" April shouted.

"Fuck you!" He growled.

"Look, man, you got this all wrong. We were talking." *Is this really happening? Unbelievable.*

"You were talking yourself into her pants."

"Seriously?" Alana joined in.

Michael glanced over and shook his head, hoping to discourage her from saying the wrong thing.

"Raul, you're overreacting," Jared said.

"Overreacting? You wouldn't say that if this

asshole was making the moves on your girl."

The nerves at the nape of Michael's neck tingled as his anger grew. "I think you've had too much to drink. Maybe you should go sleep it off."

"Oh, I'll sleep it off all right, after I've stomped your ass into the dirt." He lunged for Michael, but in an instant, Jared jumped up and punched him right in the face sending him flying backward over the sleeping bag and landing with a thud in the dirt.

"Raul?" April cried out. She pushed away from Michael and ran to him.

Michael stood there, shocked and unable to move. *Holy shit!*

Raul struggled to get up. He grabbed April by the shoulder and pushed her aside. By the time he'd gotten to his feet, Joel stood shoulder to shoulder with Jared between Michael and Raul.

"That's enough, Raul. We're all friends here," Joel said. "Michael's right. You've been drinking all day, and you didn't see whatever it was you think you saw. Mike's not after April, okay?"

"Tell *him* to say it." Raul sneered.

Jared eased to the side and Michael walked toward them. "Dude, I'm not after April. She and I were seriously only talking." Michael extended his hand as a sign of good faith. "I swear."

Raul glared at the offered hand, then eyed the group. His face darkened, and deep creases stretched across his forehead. "Maybe I have had a bit too much to drink, man. I'm sorry."

"A man shouldn't have to apologize for defending someone he cares about," Michael said. "So don't be a dick and fuck it up, okay?"

Raul shook his hand. "For reals man, you should be more careful with all that southern charm crap you're always spewing. The chicks go crazy over it."

Michael laughed. "Maybe you should try some of that charm yourself sometime, *ese*."

Raul turned around and helped April up from the ground. "I'm sorry, baby."

April hugged him, and they both walked back toward the house arm and arm.

"Damn, Prophet, you struck like a cobra. I never saw it coming." Joel patted Jared on the back.

Jared shrugged. "Raul may be my friend, but he was being a douche." He glanced over at Michael then reached down, grabbed his can of beer and headed toward the house.

Alana sidled up to Michael. "Speaking of defending someone he cares about…"

Michael peered down at her. *Humph?* "You think?"

Her face lit up with the enthusiasm of a little kid on Christmas morning. "Ooh, yeah."

TYLER ROBBINS

Chapter Eight

The entire house vibrated as thunder boomed outside. The wind whirled as badly as it had back at base earlier in the week. Tropical Storm Constance was making her presence known, and even though the lake-house was a hundred and fifty miles inland, the smaller storms that accompanied her were brutal.

Tornadoes were the biggest concern in the outlying areas, especially when a hurricane or a larger tropical storm hit. Then again, with fifty to seventy-five mile per hour winds, tropical storms destroyed as much as a tornado and on a much wider scale.

Hurricane Katrina had affected hundreds of thousands of square miles of land throughout the gulf coast, especially Louisiana. Jared had been on his first tour then, stationed in Germany. Two of the guys in his unit had family in New Orleans, and one of them had lost an uncle and a cousin when the levee broke.

Very few people who'd ever ridden out a hurricane or severe tropical storm took Mother Nature for granted after that, including Jared. His father, on the other hand, was one of the stubborn people who preferred to take life into his own hands. He'd been lucky so far, and Jared hoped his father's luck would last.

Jared stared out the living room window at what had been the campfire he'd built a few hours earlier. Rain began to fall, so faint puffs of steam drifted up every few minutes as heavy drops saturated what remained of the embers.

"How bad is it?" Michael asked as he turned over on the sofa and sat up.

Jared had been content to watch him as he slept. He wanted so badly to wake him, hold the man in his arms and drown out the rest of the world, but the instant he saw him lying there looking like an angel, peaceful and gorgeous, he let him be.

His heart skipped a beat now at the sound of his lover's voice.

"It's picking up steam."

"Did you ever reach your mom?"

Jared shook his head. "Voicemail picked up every time I called. Maybe the lines were already down." At least Jared hoped that was the problem.

Right now Jared needed a distraction, and Michael would do the trick.

Michael extended his arms over his head, and Jared's groin tingled at the sight of his treasure trail leading up to his navel from under his boxers. Michael's smooth chest rose and fell as he inhaled deeply and moaned from his extensive stretch.

"Feel better?"

A cocky grin spread across Michael's face. "I could."

Jared gazed at him, nearly hypnotized. Michael's broad shoulders, tapered waist and perfectly rounded ass, were arousing enough, but his big brown eyes and movie-star good looks pushed him over the top. On a scale of one to ten, Michael Crest was easily an eleven. How stupid had Jared been to have ignored him all those weeks before the night in the rec room? He'd tortured himself needlessly.

"Come here," Michael whispered.

Jared went to sofa and stood over him. "You're not playing fair."

Michael slipped his hand inside the front of his boxers, and Jared's mouth watered.

"Sexy mother-fucker." Jared clenched his jaw.

Michael pulled his dick from his shorts and

stroked it. He bit his bottom lip and moved his hand up and down the length of his shaft. "You know you want me."

"I know you want me to want you." Jared forced himself to resist.

"Come on. Take it."

Jared glanced toward the hallway. Anyone could walk out at any moment. "No."

"They're all asleep. We're totally alone."

Michael was probably right, but Jared had another reason for resisting. He slowly shook his head and held his breath. *Make him wait,* he thought. *Better yet, make him beg.*

Michael cupped his balls and rubbed them, making his dick bobble against his hand. "Mmm." He pressed his head into the sofa cushion. "Feels so good."

He definitely wasn't playing fair.

Jared drew in a deep breath then suddenly recalled the popsicles he'd bought at the store. That would cool him off for sure. He stepped back and headed for the kitchen.

"You're kidding right?" Michael lifted his head as Jared glanced back at him. "Jared?"

"Shh." Jared raised his hand to caution Michael. "You're gonna wake everybody up."

Michael relented and laid his head back on the sofa cushion.

A surge of cold air pelted Jared's face as he grabbed a cherry flavored Popsicle from the freezer and unwrapped it. When he returned to the living room, he sat down on the coffee table across from Michael. Using the tip of his tongue, he licked the icy treat.

Michael squirmed, then reached out and brought Jared's hand to his mouth and shoved the entire Popsicle inside. He pulled it back out and grinned. "This could have been your dick."

Jared chuckled, unzipped his jeans and freed his now engorged cock. "Oh, it will be."

Michael sat up and took the frozen treat from Jared, then slid it over his lips until they glistened red even in the darkened room.

Jared scrutinized his every move. Leaning back, he gripped the base of his cock and clenched his ass muscles, forcing his dick to jump. "Somebody's jealous."

"Somebody?" Michael chortled. He shoved the Popsicle deep into his mouth making sure to coat the inside of his cheeks and tongue with freezing cherry sweetness.

When Michael switched from the Popsicle to Jared's cock, Jared almost came right there. Electricity slammed across his body as chills bombarded his flesh. "That shit's cold."

"Almost as cold as your heart, Jared Prophet."

Jared grabbed him by the back of the head and kissed him hard. "I'm done fuckin' around." He rose from the table and strolled across the room. "You comin' or not?"

He heard Michael scramble into the bedroom behind him, and the instant Michael shut the door, Jared pinned him to the wall. His cock throbbed against Michael's hip. He had to have him. Waiting any longer wasn't an option. "How much pain are you in?"

"Pain? What pain?"

"That's what I thought." Jared glanced over his shoulder. "Don't move." He fumbled in the dark for the nightstand and whipped out a condom so fast it was a blur. A generous squirt of lube later and he pressed into Michael's back and panted into his hear. "You gotta stop fucking with these girls in front of me."

"Girls?"

"Dancing and sweet talking. They don't know you, not the real you, so you have to stop flirting."

Michael laughed. "You're jealous of a couple of girls?"

Jared reached around him and cupped Michael's balls then began to stroke his cock. "Do you ever think about fucking a girl?" Why he even asked puzzled him, but for some inexplicable reason, he had to know.

Michael shook his head. "Girls have never been my thing."

"What *is* your thing, Crest?"

Michael spun around and gripped Jared's shoulder, pulling his face close to his. "*You're* my thing."

Grabbing both of Michael's wrists with one hand, Jared stretched them above his head, pinning them against the wall. "Don't tease me."

Michael gazed up at him through hooded eyes. "I can say the same thing to you."

Jared kissed him hard, plunging his tongue deep into Michael's mouth, then asserted his strength and flipped him around again. He smeared the lubricant from his condom-covered dick onto his fingers then scraped them lightly between Michael's ass cheeks. "I'll be gentle."

At first he ran the head of his prick up and down the crack of Michael's ass, but Michael arched his back and made his ass stick out farther.

"Are you sure?" The last thing Jared wanted was a repeat of the previous night's injury.

Michael nodded eagerly. "Please?"

The desperate sound of his voice sent shivers spiraling up and down Jared's spine.

Michael must have wanted him so badly, it didn't even matter if it hurt, and as scared as Jared was that he might cause Michael pain, it seemed as though refusing would hurt worse. Jared understood that feeling all too well. In fact, he'd never understood anything more. No matter how badly it hurt to admit he had feelings for Michael, denying it any longer was unbearable.

Bracing against the wall, Jared steadied himself with his arm outstretched over Michael's shoulder. He gently guided the head inside, inching his way deeper at a slow, steady pace.

Kissing Michael's back, he felt the muscles relax, and then Michael began to writhe with an increasing rhythm until Jared was balls deep and moving his cock from side to side within him. Making love to Michael was the most thrilling thing he'd ever known, and the subtle sounds of Michael's obvious pleasure only sent blood rushing to engorge his cock even more.

No matter what Tiffany or any other woman had ever done, Michael Crest put them all to shame simply by reacting naturally to Jared's movements. They fit together like two halves of an apple, united by one single core. Whatever this was between them was inexplicable.

"I want to see you," Jared breathed into Michael's ear.

He removed himself slowly, and then Michael turned and faced him. Their cocks rubbed together, and Jared kissed Michael's neck. The exhilarating feel of Michael's body against his took Jared's breath away.

Michael kissed back and sucked Jared's ear, nibbling a little, igniting a chain reaction of gooseflesh skittering across his body.

"How do you know me so well?"

Michael lightly pinched the flesh on the back of Jared's neck. "I don't know. It's like your body whispers to mine, and then it's like—"

"Fucking magic." Jared growled then kissed Michael again. It was like magic. Jared had fallen under

Michael's spell. One he hoped was never broken.

Jared backed toward the bed and sat down taking Michael's dick into his hands. Jared fondled him and kissed his stomach with more tenderness than he'd ever shown another person in his life.

Michael caressed his head and neck in return, and somewhere in the middle of all the passion and tenderness, emotions that had been trapped deep inside of Jared burst open like fireworks on New Year's Eve. Unable to contain it, he wrapped his arms around Michael's waist and buried his head into the other man's stomach. Before he realized it, Jared began to cry.

Michael dropped to his knees and wedged himself between Jared's legs. "What's wrong? What is it?"

Jared shook his head and wiped away the falling tears. "Nothing." He sniffled.

"Jared, you can trust me."

Jared scooted back onto the bed, and Michael joined him. "I know I can, but it's something that I've never told another soul." Memories Jared had tucked away deep in the recesses of his mind bled through, one painful event at a time, catching him off guard. If he'd had a little warning, he'd have fought harder to push them back, but now it was too late.

Michael laced his fingers between Jared's. "Whenever you're ready, I'm here."

The words clanked around in his head. *Am I ready?* What would happen if he explained himself? Would Michael see him differently? Would he be so disappointed in him that he'd walk away?

Jared had to risk it. If he didn't, it would only eat away at him until there was nothing left to give Michael or anyone else for that matter. "I want to explain. I need to tell you why I have such a hard time being myself."

"Okay."

Jared's hands began to tremble, and his stomach twisted into a thousand tiny little knots, tormenting him with a treacherous ache. Could he do this or not?

"Mike." Jared looked into Michael's eyes struggling to catch his breath. "You're not the first guy I've been with. Hell, you aren't even the second."

Michael eased back. His grip on Jared's hand loosened for a second; then he squeezed it tight. "That's okay. I don't care." He nodded.

Jared searched his big brown eyes, looking for any sign that Michael might not want to hear the rest, but there was nothing more than the same warm, accepting eyes Michael always looked at him with. "It's not what you think. It has to do with what I mentioned about when I was younger. I was twelve, and there was this guy, my neighbor. He was in high school, and we used to play catch in his back yard when my dad was too busy."

Michael sat quietly holding his hand, listening.

Jared's leg began to shake as his nerves stretched to the limit. He couldn't stop now. "Sometimes I would stay the night, you know, because I looked up to him. He was the big brother I never had, and…well…my dad was always so busy, and when he wasn't busy, he never wanted do sports stuff."

Bile jutted up into the back of Jared's throat, and he swallowed hard to force it down.

"Take your time." Michael caressed the back of Jared's hand with his thumb, soothing away enough fear for Jared to continue.

"One night he told me that I was special and that he liked me." He glared at the floor then snapped his gaze back to Michael. "And by that he meant he *liked* me."

Michael nodded his head as though he understood.

"One thing led to another, and he sort of showed

me stuff. Mostly he made me do stuff to him, and sometimes he – he did to me what I did to you."

Michael cocked his head to the side as confusion seemed to take hold. "What do you mean?"

Jared's bottom lip quivered and tears welled, stinging his eyes. "He made me bleed."

Michael exhaled a heady breath. "Jared, I—"

"That's not all." Jared rose from the bed and began to pace back and forth. He had to get it all out. Michael had to know how fucked up he was before Jared could ever continue to be with him in the way they had been the last few days. "He had a buddy, and sometimes they invited me over. And the three of us played *games*. It happened so many times I lost count until they graduated high school and I went to junior high."

Jared eyed Michael up and down. What was he thinking? Was he as disgusted with him the way Jared had been disgusted with himself all these years? "Well?"

Michael peered up at him from where he still sat on the bed. "You do realize that what they did to you was wrong, right?"

Jared shook his head. "But sometimes I liked it, Michael."

"It was sex, Jared. Of course you liked it. Your body reacted the way it was supposed to. I'm not talking about your physical reaction. I'm talking about your emotional reaction."

"Isn't it all the same?"

Michael walked over to him and took his hand. "No. It's not. Look, after you did stuff with them, how did you feel?"

"I would have preferred them pissing on me and leaving me alone."

"See?" Michael smoothed his hand over Jared's chest. "Your body reacted the way your brain told it to, but your brain doesn't operate your heart. Not in the emotional sense and that's what counts. You aren't whatever it is you've thought you were all these years. *You* didn't do anything wrong, Jared. They did."

"I'm trying to see it your way, but it's hard. They made me gay whether I wanted to be or not."

Michael's brow pinched taut. "You really believe that?"

Jared struggled to rationalize it. "If they hadn't have introduced me to what they did, I would be straight, and there wouldn't be any bullshit to worry about."

"Oh, so you really get off on girls?"

"Fuck yeah!" His heart pounded in his chest the instant he blurted the half-truth.

"Really?"

Jared went back to the bed. He couldn't lie to Michael, and he knew it. Even worse, Michael knew it, too. "No." He relented, wringing his hands. "Not like I get off on you."

"Am I the only guy you've ever been attracted to?"

Jared's face burned hot. "No, but you are the only guy I've…acted on it with as an adult."

"So," Michael folded his arms across his chest, and an air of smugness sifted over him. "I'm your first."

The mood lightened quickly. Jared chuckled at the way Michael appeared so pleased with himself. "Okay, when you put it the way you're putting it, then yes, you, Michael Crest are my first… whatever."

Michael licked his lips as a satisfied grin spread across his face. "What was that? Your first what?"

"My first man… er… lover… fuck, I don't even know what in the hell to call you."

Michael sauntered over to him and pushed him back onto the bed. "I don't care what you call me, just as long as you do." He kissed Jared softly and straddled him in the middle of the bed. "You can't undo the bad stuff, but you can try to fill your life with good things. It's not easy, but I believe you can get past this."

When Michael said it, Jared almost believed it. Maybe he would get past it. Maybe his life didn't have to be ruined by what happened.

"Now," Michael said. "Can we finish what we started or not?"

Jared flipped him over and engulfed Michael's mouth with his, making deep sweeps with his tongue, tangling it around Michael's.

"Make love to me," Michael whispered.

He didn't have to ask twice.

TYLER ROBBINS

Chapter Nine

Rain pounded the roof at a near deafening level. The storm had escalated, adding to the intensity of the event occurring between Jared and Michael.

Michael knelt on all fours, and the pain from the previous night was nothing more than a distant memory as Jared gripped his hips and grinded into him. Nothing remained but pleasure like he'd never known.

He stroked himself, increasing the thrill as Jared filled him with the full girth of his prick.

If what Michael felt for Jared wasn't love, he didn't know what to call it. It was definitely more than anything he'd ever felt for anyone before and had certainly exceeded mere fascination.

"Turn over," Jared instructed as he withdrew himself from Michael's ass.

Michael did as he asked and flipped onto his back.

Jared stretched over him and began kissing his neck while rubbing Michael's cock. "You're amazing."

"I'm amazing?" Michael chuckled. "I think you mean *you're* amazing."

"Yeah, I kind of am." Jared laughed then kissed him again.

Michael caressed Jared's chest, savoring every inch of him. Jared's nipple poked his palm, and Michael flicked it with his tongue as he ventured down Jared's body. He skimmed his tongue over Jared's hip bones then made his way to his cock and balls.

He lifted Jared's hips and tongued his asshole, licking and probing as deep as possible.

Jared moaned.

Michael spat onto his fingers and moistened the area, while lapping wildly at the hole, kissing and nibbling the soft skin between Jared's ass cheeks and up and down his inner thighs.

"Shit. That feels so good." Jared panted.

Michael already knew that. Jared had been pleasuring him this way for days, and he wanted to return the favor. He longed to feel his cock deep within Jared, but had yet to actually make it happen.

Somehow, Jared managed to take over and make love to him, but now it was finally Michael's turn.

He teased Jared's hole with the tip of his finger, switching back and forth between his tongue and fingertip.

Jared writhed on the bed.

Michael inserted his finger almost to his knuckle, and Jared instantly clamped down, preventing Michael from going deeper.

"Relax, baby."

Jared took Michael's hand and pulled it back then swung his leg over Michael's head, and rolled over onto his side. "Give me a minute."

Michael rose up onto his knees. "I want to make love to you."

Jared looked back over his shoulder. "I know, but I need a minute. I'm not ready."

Michael lay down on the bed behind him and held Jared close. He rested his chin on the curve of Jared's neck. "I'm in no hurry." And he wasn't.

After what Jared had revealed about being violated as a young boy, Michael should have known better. Shit, he could hardly blame him. If that had happened to him, he'd probably never want another guy's hands on him at all.

"I'm sorry."

"No need to apologize. I get it."

A loud crashing noise slammed against the

window, and Jared lifted his head and looked to where it resonated. "It's getting bad out there."

Michael kissed his shoulder. "Yeah, but it's dry in here."

"Hey, if I asked you something personal, would you tell me?"

"You can ask me anything."

"Did you mean it when you said you've never liked girls?"

Michael hadn't expected the question, but the answer was pretty easy. "I thought I liked a girl once and even considered messing around to test myself."

"Test yourself?"

"Yeah, I mean boys always caught my attention, even as a kid, but I thought maybe I should be with a girl to see if I felt the same for both or if it was only for boys."

"What did you find?" Jared turned over and faced him.

"I was friends with this older guy named Jake who had a sister, Jennifer. She was really pretty, and all my friends were crazy about her, but Jennifer liked me."

"A real Casanova." Jared grinned.

"Exactly." Michael winked. "Well one day Jennifer and I were alone, and she kissed me. Don't get me wrong. It was a nice kiss, but while her tongue was halfway down my throat, all I thought of was Jake."

Jared's eyes widened. "Her brother? Man, that must have been awkward as hell."

"Yeah, especially since I already had an idea Jake liked me, too."

"Did you and he ever…?"

Michael shook his head. "We spent a lot of time together, and when we were alone camping, he held my hand while we talked all night long."

"So neither of you ever acted on it?"

"He kissed me one time, the night before he moved away for college, and I haven't seen him since."

"He left? Just like that?"

"He told me the world wouldn't understand, and we'd be better off if we both forgot how we felt and did what everyone else did. Get married, have kids and find a way to be happy."

Jared's eyes narrowed, and he seemed to stare off into nothing. "He sounds a lot like me." He rolled onto his back, grabbed his pack of cigarettes from the nightstand and lit one. The end glowed bright in the dark as he inhaled.

Michael rose up on his elbow. "He's nothing like you."

Unexpectedly, Jared pressed the butt of the cigarette to Michael's lips, and he took a drag off of it, as well. The filter was still damp from where Jared's lips had held it. The gesture wasn't a big thing, but the idea of Jared taking care of Michael without a second thought, even as corny as sharing the same cigarette, made Michael feel even more connected to him.

"I tried to pretend." Jared said. "Hell, I've been with more girls than most guys my age, trying to find someone capable of making me feel something…anything really."

"I thought about doing that and even tried, but every time I found myself getting close to a girl, they'd eventually ask me what it's like being gay."

"They all knew?"

"Every last one of them. I used to wonder if I was too feminine, but Alana told me there's something about me she connects to in a way she's only connected with her girlfriends. Of course, she calls it *gay-dar*." He laughed.

"Joel's Alana?"

"Yep, I actually introduced them. Joel and I had been roommates about a month when I met her. They hooked up and have been together ever since."

"Humph." Jared puffed the cigarette again. "What does Joel think about all this?"

"He's my friend. If I'm happy, he's happy."

"And you two never—"

Michael shook his head. "He's straight, and I would never cross that line."

"You crossed it with me."

"You were never straight."

"You didn't know that." Jared sat up and leaned against the headboard.

"Didn't I?"

"How?" His eyes widened with obvious interest.

"That night in the bathroom stall. When I looked down at you, your eyes sort of lit up, and then when you grabbed my arm, you held it a bit longer than you should have."

Jared stared at him but didn't say a word.

"When we were running in the woods and you stopped to make your little declaration about not needing distractions, I knew you were struggling to fight whatever attraction you had. That's why I did what I did when you kissed me. I knew that if you walked away, you'd keep lying."

"So you figured giving me head would wake me up?" Jared laughed.

"Did it?"

"No. I didn't wake up completely until I saw you changing clothes in the bathroom. When I saw you naked, my dick got so hard I thought I would pass out from the blood loss to the rest of my body. I had to have you."

Michael kissed Jared's chest. "And have me you did."

Jared rubbed Michael's shoulder. "I want to give myself to you like that, too. I need some time."

Michael leaned his head into Jared's arm as he caressed his shoulder. "Like I said, I'm not going anywhere."

A loud clap of thunder rattled the window pane, and Michael jumped. "Fuck. That was loud."

Jared laughed. He put the cigarette out in the ashtray, flipped Michael onto his back and covered his body with his. "I'll protect you, baby."

Michael struggled under the weight of Jared's larger frame to get the upper hand, but Jared had pinned him so fast there was nothing he could do. Jared's instant domination excited him, and Michael became immediately aroused. His dick jammed up into Jared's stomach.

"Goddamn, Crest? Are you trying to stab me with that thing?"

Michael jutted his chin upward, hoping Jared would kiss him, and naturally, Jared didn't disappoint.

Jared's tongue dove deep, and Michael sucked it as enthusiastically as he had sucked Jared's cock.

When Jared lifted his head he gazed down into Michael's eyes so intently, Michael's whole body shuddered from the effects of whatever emotion Jared exuded.

"I think I could fall in love with you," Michael whispered.

Jared smiled and kissed him again.

Lightning flashed outside, filling the room with light, and then another ground trembling blast of thunder shook the whole house and was followed by a crash that sounded more like a car smashing through the wall.

"What was that?" Michael asked.

Jared shook his head and started to get upright as the bedroom door swung open and banged against the wall.

Raul's voice bellowed at the top of his lungs, "A tree fell on the – what the fuck?"

Jared jumped to his feet, taking the bed sheet with him, leaving Michael in the bed naked. Michael looked over at Raul whose expression had transformed into a mixture of shock and disgust. "What the fuck?" he repeated.

Jared stood in front of Raul, his face as pallid as a ghost. He'd never looked more vulnerable in all the time Michael had known him.

Michael's heart pounded as he got to his feet and grabbed his jeans from the floor by the bed. "A tree fell on what?" he asked as he pulled his jeans up and fastened them.

"Were you fuckin' him?" Raul glared at Jared with his head tilted to the side and a grimace so contorted he really did look like a bulldog. *"Pinche maricón."*

"What did you say?" April's voice rang out above the constant clamor of thunder.

"A tree fell on the house, and these two *jotos* are in here fucking!"

"That's it!" Michel jumped over the bed and charged Raul, clipping him at the waist, slamming him back onto the hallway floor. He straddled him and pounded Raul's face with clenched fists while deflecting Raul's attempts to punch back.

"Michael!" Alana screamed. "Stop. You're gonna kill him."

Michael ignored Alana's pleas. He'd wanted to deck Raul for two days already, and this was his shot. "It's none of your goddamn business." Pain blasted his knuckles as his fist made direct contact with Raul's mouth. Blood splattered everywhere.

Michael threw another punch as he felt himself being lifted from under his arms, and Joel's voice grumbled his ear. "That's enough. You made your point."

"Let go of me, goddammit!" Michael squirmed and struggled to break Joel's hold.

"Mikey." Alana's sweet voice resonated over the commotion, bringing him back to his senses. "Please, stop."

Michael collapsed onto floor. He huffed and dragged in one ragged breath after another trying his best to calm down.

"Go make sure Raul's conscious," Joel said.

Alana joined April, and they both knelt next to Raul. "He's okay."

"Get him into the other room and take care of his fucking face."

Michael crawled over to the bed and pulled himself up to his knees. Blood dripped from his hands, and the pain from his bruised ribs returned. He held his chest and tried to take a deep breath, but wheezed instead. He'd probably done more than bruise them this time. He'd more than likely cracked them. "Fuck."

"What in the hell happened?" Joel stood over him.

"He busted through the door saying something about a tree, and then all hell broke loose."

Joel helped him to the bed. "Where's Jared?"

Michael looked around the room. "Hell, he was right here."

"He probably went to see if there's any permanent damage to Raul's face."

Michael glanced up at Joel, his ears still ringing. "How will you be able to tell?"

Joel laughed. "The little guy sure learned the hard

way why nobody ever wants to spar with you."

"He fucking pissed me off."

"You know you could have really hurt him."

"I meant to hurt him."

"Yeah, that's what you need, a few months in the stockade for assaulting a fellow soldier. Not to mention whatever other charges they might slap on for the hell of it to make an example out of you."

"He's not my fellow soldier."

"The hell he's not. Like it or not, he's your brother."

"Fuck him." Michael had no intentions of backing down.

"Okay. I see we're gonna have to agree to disagree. I'm gonna go get some ice for that hand." Joel headed for the door, but stopped as he reached it. "For what it's worth, I'd have knocked the hell out of him, too, if he'd said those things to me."

Michael cradled his midsection and reached for his shirt on the floor. He pulled it over his head and went into the bathroom. Peering into the mirror, he noticed a deep scratch across his right brow. He turned on the water faucet and splashed water on his face.

"Here, let me see how bad that is," Alana said from the bathroom doorway. "Sit."

Michael didn't argue. He sat on the closed toilet and looked up at her.

"You and your damn temper."

"I had a good reason to beat his ass."

"I know." She dabbed his eyebrow with the cloth she'd brought with her. "But you forget that all that combat training is supposed to be used on the enemy, not other army personnel."

"I knew how to fight long before the army trained me for anything." He winced as she pressed harder on his cut. "Try growing up gay in a small Texas town. The other kids knew about my fighting skills; otherwise they'd have kicked my ass every day."

"Your dad was a smart man." Alana mussed his hair.

"My dad knew his son. He also knew I would have it rough."

"Did he tell you that?"

"He didn't have to. My sexuality was the elephant in the room we all knew about, but never made a fuss over."

"I guess with an only child they were grateful you were healthy and happy."

Michael couldn't argue with her there. Not everyone was that lucky. "If only Jared had it that easy."

"Where is he anyway?"

Michael nudged her back and clutched his side as a sharp pain reminded him of his injury. "Wasn't he in the living room with y'all?"

"The last time I saw him was when Joel dragged you off of Raul."

"Shit. I better find him." Michael headed for the living room.

Raul sat in a chair while April applied an ice pack to his jaw.

Michael overlooked the battered man and eyed Joel. "Where is he?"

"I have no idea."

"He wasn't even dressed, Michael. He zoomed past me in the hallway wrapped in that sheet," April said.

"He wouldn't have been in that goddamned sheet if they'd have kept their fuckin' dicks in their pants." Raul glared up at Michael.

Michael stepped closer. "How would you like me to bitch slap your sorry ass again?"

Raul jumped to his feet. "Bring it, *maricón.*"

April jumped up and wedged her tiny body between the two men. "Have you lost your mind, you big asshole?" She stood toe to toe with Raul, her hands planted firmly on her hips.

Michael balled his fists, ready to pick up where he'd left off.

"How did you get away with it all this time anyway? Must have sucked a lot of cock to move your way up the ranks?" Raul obviously wasn't backing down.

"If you make one more comment about his sexuality, I swear to God, I'm outta here," April said.

Raul looked down at her. "Baby, are you defending him?"

"Damn straight I am." April turned and faced Michael with tears welling in her eyes. "If more people stood up for what's right, then maybe my older brother would still be around."

"What? You have an older brother?" Raul's demeanor changed as April revealed something he obviously hadn't known.

"*Had.* I *had* a brother. He was gay, and my parents couldn't deal with it. He couldn't either, and when it got too much, he stopped the pain the only way he knew. He wrapped his motorcycle around a tree."

"He killed himself?" Alana asked. "I never knew." She went over and hugged her friend.

"Nobody did. Until now." She turned to Raul. "I'd give anything to have him back. A gay brother sure beats the hell out of a dead brother any day."

The hair on Michael's neck stood on end. "I'm sorry for your loss, April, I really am." His attention then changed back to Raul. "In case you didn't know it, don't ask, don't tell was repealed, so I didn't have to hide anything from any one. I have as much right to privacy as you do, so it's none of your business or anyone else's who I date."

"What about my right not to worry about one of you people trying to fuck with me?" Raul bowed his chest up.

"Seriously?" Joel said. "I knew you weren't all that bright, but I never took you for a complete idiot."

"He's your roommate." Raul stepped toward Joel in a confrontational manner and eyed him up and down. "You fucking him, too?"

Michael's muscles tightened as he mentally prepared to defend his friend.

Joel held up his hand to thwart Michael's impending approach, then glared at Raul. "Every chance I get."

Michael eased back and bit back the laughter that threatened release. Had he heard Joel right?

"Joel, shut up." Alana laughed, instead. "You're not helping." She stepped in front of Joel and confronted Raul as well. "The point is that it's none of your business who's doing who. We don't want to know about your sex life, and you don't need to know about theirs."

Raul shook his head. "I didn't want to know. I found out by accident."

"Because you burst into Jared's room like a mad man." Michael's jaw tensed.

"I thought a tree had crashed through the house."

"Well it hadn't," April said. "I tried to tell you it was a fallen limb, but you had already run off like a crazy man."

"I wouldn't have gone into the room if I had known they were…" His expression contorted again. "Doing what they were doing." Raul sat back down looking more and more like a pouting three year old than the bulldog Michael had kicked the hell out of.

"Listen, y'all can stand around here and deal with him all you want, but I need to find Jared." Michael made a beeline for the door.

"Wait, I'll come, too." Joel followed behind.

They stepped outside into the dark. Heavy rain made it difficult for Michael to make out the shape of the pier or even the lake off in the distance. "I have an idea where he may be, but maybe you should check out the lake and the boat shed. If you don't find him, don't worry about me. I'll be okay," he shouted over the deafening sound of the pouring rain.

Joel nodded and headed toward the lake.

Michael wiped the streaming water from his face and trekked toward where Jared had taken him the first day they arrived. His old fort.

The woods looked much different in the torrential downpour, but Michael's instincts as a soldier kicked in, and he recalled certain distinctive things about the trail his mind had naturally noted.

The fort stood about two hundred meters past the white oak tree at the forest's edge. He looked for the two fallen pine trees crisscrossing like an X about twenty feet in the air. Damn. Had he really remembered all that from one trip?

Wind gusts blew tree branches and leaves whirling around Michael, assaulting his face and arms with sharp needlelike pricks. As he neared the leaning pines, he shouted, "Jared!"

No sign of him. "Jared?"

A tree branch snapped behind him, and Michael turned to find Jared standing next to a pile of what had been his childhood fort.

"It's all gone," he yelled back.

"We need to get inside." Michael advanced toward him. "I told you we'd rebuild it, and we will."

"No, it's all over, man." Jared's distraught expression sent swirls of nausea into a tailspin deep within Michael's gut.

"Let's go, Jared."

"I can't do this. I'm no good for you, Michael."

Michael grabbed his arm. "Let me decide what's good for me."

Jared jerked away. "When the storm passes, I want you to go. All of you."

Michael pulled the twisted sheet from around Jared's waist, then shook it out and wrapped it back around him. "We'll discuss this inside where it's safe."

"No, goddammit! Listen to me!"

Michael paused. The desperation in Jared's tone worried him.

"Give me your word that as soon as this storm passes you'll go back to the base and do whatever you have to do to stay away from me."

"No."

Jared gripped Michael's upper arms and shoved him back. "If you don't leave me alone, I'll only fuck your life up."

Michael pushed back and broke the hold Jared had on him. "Nobody tells me what to do, Prophet. Not you, not Raul, and damn sure not the rest of the fucking world."

Water drenched them both as torrents of rain soaked them through and through. "Come back, and we'll talk about it."

"I'll come back, but my mind is made up."

It really didn't matter what Jared said. He was upset and for good reason. Shock and fear were talking now, and if Michael stood by him, they'd make it through the rough patch.

The truth would inevitably come out, and Michael

cared enough to help Jared no matter what it cost.

He led Jared back into the house and ignored everyone as they entered.

Alana stood and looked as though she would come toward them, but Michael waved her away.

Jared's silence troubled him. How long could someone remain in shock before it became dangerous?

After they entered the bedroom, Michael dried Jared off and helped him into bed.

His stomach twisted, and the uneasy feeling he'd had that night he and Jared smoked in the bathroom of the rec center, slowly returned. A dull ache settled into his gut, and this time Michael knew without a doubt. Something bad was heading their way.

TYLER ROBBINS

Chapter Ten

Bright sunlight penetrated the curtain sheers to Jared's parents' bedroom. His whole body ached, and for an instant, he wondered why as he sat up and gathered his senses. His pounding head didn't help.

He instinctively reached for Michael, but the bed beside him remained empty and cold. Panicked, Jared sprang up and scanned the room only to find Michael lying on the floor against the wall with his head propped up on his duffel bag.

Had he slept there all night? "Mike." His scratchy throat stung.

No response.

"Michael," he raised his voice.

Michael stirred then slowly sat up and rubbed his eyes. "Cool, you're awake."

Jared reached for his clothes. "Shit, I really fucked up." An uneasy sense of anxiety gnawed in his gut.

"You didn't do anything."

"I ran out of here like a pussy. I'm sorry."

Michael got to his feet and joined Jared on the bed. "You were upset."

"That's no excuse. I've gotta deal with this. Shit, I should have dealt with this a long time ago."

Michael rubbed Jared's shoulder. "It's all gonna work out."

Jared got up and collected his clothes. The fear he'd felt the night before had faded, and now anger gradually took its place. "I need to settle up with Raul."

"You don't owe him an explanation."

Jared pulled his t-shirt over his head. "No, I'm not cool with what he said, and he needs to hear it from me."

Nodding, as if in agreement, Michael walked into the bathroom.

"Have you heard anything about the storm?" Jared called out, his voice becoming stronger.

"No. I think Joel has the radio, though," Michael said back over the sound of running water.

Jared pulled his jeans on and then his shoes. "I need to call my parents again."

Michael emerged from the bathroom with water beading across his tanned body, looking downright irresistible.

Jared's gaze roamed over every muscle of his abdomen and bare chest. When his eyes settled on Michael's big brown orbs, his scalp tingled. "What the hell?" He stalked over to the other man and examined the cut over his brow, diligently tilting Michael's head from side to side.

"You should see the other guy."

Jared mulled over the events from the previous night and recalled Michael's ferocious assault of Raul after – well, after shit went sideways. "I never meant for any of that to go down that way."

"Jared, it's nobody's fault. It just happened."

Jared nodded, if only to avoid an argument. If he'd been more of a man and less of a coward, Michael wouldn't have had to tackle Raul at all. "At least now I know you can handle yourself without me."

"What?" Michael looked up at him with a severely arched brow. "Did you think I needed protecting?"

"No," Jared said, suddenly realizing how his comment may have sounded a bit condescending.

"I'm a big boy, Jared. I've dealt with dumbass haters my whole life."

"I know, I only meant…" He struggled for the

words.

"You meant what?"

Jared sighed. What in the hell did he mean? Was Michael the type of man who needed to be taken care of, or did Jared naturally want to take care of him whether Michael wanted him to or not? He wasn't a girl. Fuck! *Am I supposed to* want *to protect him at all?* Confusing thoughts stacked in his mind. "Hell, I don't know." He pulled his t-shirt over his head. "I have to deal with my own dumbass hater right now, and then see what's going on with my parents."

He'd figure it all out later, after dealing with the fallout with Raul.

"Sure, man."

Jared walked toward the bedroom door, but turned and went back over to Michael. "Thanks for not giving up on me."

Michael skimmed his fingers across Jared's hand. "I gave you my word that we'd figure this out."

Jared leaned in and kissed Michael's cheek then left him standing there alone.

The length of the hallway grew longer with each nerve-racking step toward the living room. Jared breathed a sigh of relief when he found only Alana and April on the sofa listening to the radio.

Both greeted him with enthusiastic smiles.

"Good morning, handsome." Alana spoke first.

"Need some coffee?" April asked.

"No thanks, I'm good." His cheeks were warm from embarrassment. They'd seen much more of him than he would have preferred the night before and knew far more about him than any other women had ever known, including his own mother. "I'm sorry about last night."

Alana looked up at him and grinned. "Don't

apologize. Last night was like a dream come true for me."

"A dream come true?" What did she mean by that?

"Oh, yes. I'm a big fan of boys who like boys."

"It's really hot," April said.

Jared froze. Had he heard them right? "Seriously?"

Alana jumped up and sauntered over to him. "You're both sexy as hell, and I bet the sex is phenomenal."

Jared shook his head in disbelief. "This isn't what I expected." They were so cool with it, but how? Shouldn't they be uncomfortable?

"What did you expect?" Alana asked.

"I don't know, but I never expected it to be so easy to take."

Alana laughed. "Have you seen yourself in the mirror? You're gorgeous, and so is Mikey. What's hotter than two sexy guys goin' at it all hot and heavy?"

"Two hot girls," Joel said as he walked into the room and slipped his arms around Alana's middle.

The level of embarrassment increased tenfold with Joel suddenly in the mix. Jared stepped back, allowing some space between himself and Michael's best friend.

Joel grinned down at Alana then turned toward Jared. "Glad you got some sense last night and came in the house before you got yourself killed." He stretched out his hand.

At first, Jared half-expected to burst into flames upon first contact, but instead Joel tightened his grip as they shook hands.

"Where's Michael?" Joel asked.

Jared gulped down the thick ball of air wedged in the back of his throat and pointed back toward the bedroom.

"Good, I didn't want him to go outside without me." Joel gave Alana a quick kiss. "Jared, there are some pretty big limbs down out there. We'll help you take care of 'em before we head out today."

"You're leaving?" Jared stepped toward the window to peek outside.

"Yeah, I think maybe you and Michael should hang back a couple of days. Give yourselves some time to figure things out."

Figure things out? Right. Maybe some real alone time together would shed some light on the already complicated situation. That and he really didn't want to face whomever Raul might blab to about what he'd witnessed. Jared's Army days were numbered, but he didn't want to be ground zero for a lot of gossip and ridicule until his retirement papers came through either.

He swallowed hard, knowing exactly what he had to do. "Where's Raul?" He directed the question to April.

"Down by the pier. I told him we weren't leaving until he apologized to you and Michael."

"Thanks. I'm gonna talk to him now." Jared left them in the house and headed down to the lake.

Raul squatted on the end of the pier skipping rocks across the water.

Jared couldn't say anything at first. The words hung in the back of his throat, and until he actually looked Raul in the eye, they wouldn't mean much anyway.

"Did you come to tell me what an asshole I am, too?" Raul spoke first.

"I came to apologize to you."

"Apologize? For what? For lying? For being a fraud?" Contempt seeped from his tone.

Jared's stomach flip flopped. In essence, he was

guilty of all of it. "Man, I can't explain why I couldn't admit the things going on inside my head. I'm a coward. It's that simple.

Raul remained facing away from him. "You know you were the first person to show me around when I arrived at the base." Raul's voice cracked. "I looked up to you. Hell I wanted to be you."

Jared shook his head. "Why would you want to be me?"

Raul glanced over at him with his left eye almost swollen shut and his bottom lip busted pretty badly. He looked like he'd been hit by a truck. A Mack truck named Michael.

"Fuck. You don't know what it's like to come from where I come from. A town so small and a family so poor, the army was my only way out. I actually have a shot at becoming somebody instead of a drunk like my old man with a wife who stays up all night making tamales, then goes to a second job all day to keep the electric company from shutting off the lights." He flung another rock into the water with a deep grunt. "You were nice and decent, and you didn't judge me because I'm Mexican. You treated me like I'm somebody."

Jared's ears rang as the threat of tears stung the backs of his eyes. "You are somebody."

"I come from a family of devout Catholics, and no, I'm not an angel, but I do have a sense of what's right and what's wrong and…" He narrowed his gaze. "I don't see how two guys…" He grimaced again, obviously still as disgusted as he'd been when he found Jared and Michael together. "It's not right."

Jared swallowed the bile burning the back of his throat. "I can't make you understand something I don't even understand myself. You're my friend, and I'm sorry I lied, but it had nothing to do with you."

"It does have something to do with me. For fuck's sake, I've pissed in front of you. How do I know you weren't looking at my shit when that happened? It's a violation of my privacy."

"Raul, man, it doesn't work that way. I haven't done anything to you other than not tell you my business. Shouldn't I have that right?"

"Not when you're lying about what you are."

"What I am?" Jared's blood simmered as a spark of anger flared. "I'm a goddamn human being and a damn good soldier in the United States Army. I've served my country for nearly eight years. I've had bullets flying over my head and would die for you and every other American because that's who I am and what I stand for. I'd take a bullet for you the same as any other soldier who's out in the shit. Why should it matter who I love or what makes me happy?"

Raul shook his head. "It just does." He stepped toward Jared. "I'm sorry, man, but I don't think I can overlook this. So, maybe it's best if you stay away from me." He walked past Jared, but stopped as he reached the bank a few feet away. "I won't tell people your business, but it's probably not a good idea for you to advertise it either. I'm not the only one who feels this way."

Jared remained behind. His arms and legs suddenly felt like Jell-O. He couldn't follow Raul to defend himself if he'd wanted to. Even if he did, what would he say? Would he say he understood? Would he argue how being attracted to men was as normal as Raul being in to girls? He could, but Raul's mind wasn't in a place to listen. Besides, Jared barely understood it himself.

It was best to leave well enough alone.

Jared lingered down by the lake alone until he heard the sound of Raul's truck pulling out of the driveway and heading back up the road.

When he returned to the house, he found Michael, Joel and Alana standing on the front porch. "Are y'all about to leave?"

Alana nodded. "We're waiting for April. She's in the bathroom."

Jared's heart plummeted into his stomach. "She didn't leave with Raul?"

Alana responded with a frown and a shake of her head.

He pounded the porch railing as frustration and remorse gnawed at his heart. "Are there any more relationships I can fuck up today?"

"You aren't to blame for that," Alana said reaching out with a friendly touch. "Raul is a big boy, and he can make his own mistakes."

"April told him last night what she needed from him, and he couldn't give it to her," Michael said.

Jared shook his head. What more could he say? No matter what he did, nothing good would come of the choices he'd made.

The screen door opened, and April emerged with puffy eyes. She'd been crying.

"April, I'm sorry," Jared said.

"Don't be. I made up my mind a long time ago about what I believe in, and I made a vow to my brother I would never back down or let ignorance or prejudice win." She eased up to Michael and took his hand. "You were right. He's a knuckle-dragger, and if he can't see love right in front of his face then it's his loss."

Michael kissed her forehead. "He'll come around."

She shook her head. "If he does, he does, but I'm not going to lose sleep over someone who has no respect for me or his friends."

Jared was once again blown away by the loyalty and true friendships he'd forged with the people before him. They'd only known him a few days, yet they'd been better friends to him than people he'd known his whole life. Where had they been all this time? If he had known them when he was young, would his life be so fucked up now?

He might never know the answer, but in that moment he valued each of them in a way he'd never valued other friends.

"We're going up to Alana's parents' condo for a few days," Joel said. "Michael, I'll call you later to let you know what the roads look like."

Jared had forgotten all about Tropical Storm Constance. "I'm going to try calling my parents again." He hugged the girls and shook Joel's hand. "We'll have to do this again sometime. Without all the drama, though."

"We'd like that." Alana smiled. She rose up on her tiptoes and kissed his cheek, then squeezed Michael's forearm. "Are y'all ready?"

Joel shook Jared's and Michael's hands and carted Alana off under his arm while playfully kissing her.

"It really is too bad you're not straight. I have a feeling you would have rocked my world." April laughed as she hugged Michael.

"You've already have rocked my world, simply by being in it," Michael said.

"Damn. See what I mean?" She took a deep breath and sighed. "Don't fuck him over," she said to Jared as she hugged him next.

Jared's stomach flip-flopped. He hugged her back and smiled as he and Michael watched them pile into Alana's black Dodge Charger and drive away.

Michael slipped up beside him. "Are you sure you're okay with me staying behind? I can call them to come back and pick me up."

Jared pulled him close. "Don't you fucking dare." He leaned in and kissed him softly.

Michael took him by the hand and led him back into the house.

Jared's cock twitched inside his jeans. He couldn't wait another minute. Before the door had closed all the way, he rushed Michael to the sofa and pulled him down on top of him. His tongue plunged deep into Michael's warm mouth.

"Get these fucking pants off."

Michael resisted. "You take them off me."

Jared flipped Michael over. His legs stretched down the length of the sofa. He straddled the other man and unbuttoned his jeans, rubbing Michael's already engorged prick as he moved his hand down to his crotch. "You're so fucking sexy."

Michael gazed up at him through hooded eyes. "Look who's talking." He caressed Jared's chest sending electricity surging through him.

Jared jerked down Michael's jeans, then his boxers, leaving him lying there in a navy blue t-shirt. He rose and stood next to the sofa then pulled off his own t-shirt and unfastened his pants.

Michael looked up at him with hungry eyes, dark and full of lust.

Jared grasped the base of his cock and flopped it up and down in front of Michael's face, teasing him.

Michael licked his lips, and Jared gasped the instant Michael's warm, wet mouth engulfed the head of his cock. "Mmm."

"Is that what you wanted?"

"Fuck, yeah," Jared said through gritted teeth.

Michael laughed deviously then swallowed the entire length of him leaving Jared to deal with the burning fire brewing in the pit of his stomach, savagely ripping across his body with the passionate fury of an inferno.

"Shit." Jared could hardly breathe. "Turn the fuck over."

Michael didn't budge. Instead he lifted Jared's balls and drew them into his mouth, rolling them around, sucking and probing them with his tongue. He stroked Jared's cock while diligently sucking his now slippery wet balls. Then he returned back to the shaft, licking and lapping every sensitive inch of Jared's cock.

Jared's legs buckled, and he sat back on the coffee table, prompting Michael to move to the floor to come at him from a lower vantage point.

Michael lifted one of Jared's legs and placed it over his shoulder, then did the same to the other while he continued to feverishly suck him off.

Jared's mind swam with utter pleasure, and he barely noticed when Michael's tongue invaded his ass. Tingles of excitement assaulted his stomach, and then the slight pressure of fingers followed Michael's hot tongue.

Jared held his breath as Michael's finger dove deeper, then from one sudden burst of ecstasy, Jared's body jerked. "Fuck." He opened his eyes to see Michael on his knees, one hand jammed under Jared's ass, holding him in place while the other hand did things to Jared's body he'd never imagined possible.

Michael's determined gaze penetrated Jared's mind and inched dangerously close to reaching Jared's soul.

Lifting his ass, Jared encouraged Michael to continue his mission. So when Michael gripped Jared's hips and pulled him toward him, Jared followed without protest.

"Lay on the sofa," Michael instructed between heavy pants.

Although trembling with uncertainty, Jared he did as he was told.

Resting on his knees, Michael nestled between Jared's spread legs.

Jared drew his knees to his chest and watched Michael's every move with an intense sense of anticipation.

Michael massaged Jared's asshole with the tip of his dick causing Jared's heart to pound. Michael then slid his cock upward against Jared's before spitting on all four fingertips of his right hand to wet Jared's hole. The cool sensation of moisture sent chills skittering up Jared's spine as Michael lubricated him.

Jared lifted his hips higher for easy access, grabbed his cock and stroked it, eyeing every move Michael made.

Michael bit his bottom lip. His chest heaved, and the enthusiasm between them grew. "Tell me what you want," he whispered as he slid what felt like two fingers into Jared's ass.

Jared bit back a yelp, grunting instead. "I want you inside me."

"You want what?"

Michael's teasing tone infuriated him. How could he play at a time like this? "I want you inside me!"

"Are you giving yourself to me?"

Jared's head swam with a mixture of desperation and need. "Stop playing fucking games."

Michael tilted his head to the side, and his brow pinched. Then without a word, he moved as though to get up.

Jared panicked and clutched his arm. "Don't!"

Michael shot back a cocky grin. "Then tell me."

In that instant, Jared finally understood. It wasn't a tease. Michael needed to hear it. He needed to know without a doubt that Jared wanted him. "I want you to make it all right." He gulped down a ball of tangy air lodged in the back of his throat. "I need *you* to be the one, Michael."

Michael bent over and kissed him. "I've got you."

Jared took a deep breath and ran his fingers across the back of Michael's head. "I trust you."

Michael's gaze bored deep into Jared's, and without even a flicker of regret, Jared handed himself over to the other man.

As Michael pressed his cock inside Jared's ass, Jared marveled at how easy it had been to relinquish all control to Michael, not out of fear or because he felt he had to, but because he wanted to. No. *Needed* to.

Michael gently rocked back and forth within Jared's core, kissing and caressing his skin. Jared hadn't expected the tenderness of Michael's touch, so different from the times he'd been touched in the past.

This felt pure and right.

Somewhere amidst the passion and intensity of the moment, Jared knew he'd never be the same again. No matter what happened with Raul, or what came from the secret he'd kept for so many years, his life had changed forever, and in that instant, Jared finally knew who he was.

TYLER ROBBINS

Chapter Eleven

"Yes, sir." Jared paced back and forth between the kitchen and the living room with his cell phone pressed to his ear. "I'll let you know as soon as I get there."

Michael listened to the conversation as he entered the room, towel drying his hair. Had Jared finally reached his parents?

"No, sir," Jared said as he lifted his hand to hold Michael at bay. "The moment I find them, I'll have him call you."

Maybe not.

"Yes, sir, I know it's dangerous. I'll be very careful." Jared clenched his eyes shut. "Love you, too." He closed his phone, and the expression in Jared's eyes left a tangled mess of nerves spiraling down Michael's spine.

"What is it?"

"That was my uncle. He saw a report on The Weather Channel that tornadoes leveled the area where my parents live. A day care center three blocks from my parents' house was blown to pieces, and several children are missing. No one has heard from my mom or dad." Jared sat on the edge of the coffee table and buried his face in his hands.

Michael went to him and squeezed his shoulder. "Okay. What's the plan?"

"Plan?" He got to his feet and looked around the room. "I grab some supplies, take you back to base and head to Houston."

Michael shook his head. "No, I'm coming with you."

"I can't take you to my parent's house. Hell, I don't even know if there is a house anymore."

"I'm not going home. Besides, why go four hours out of your way, to turn around and head back east? It's a straight shot down fifty-nine to Houston from here. We can make it in a couple of hours if I go, too."

"Michael, this isn't a game. My dad isn't Raul."

"I want to help, Jared. It's not like you have to walk up and introduce me as the guy you're fucking."

Jared exhaled. "I don't have time to argue." He rubbed the back of his neck. "Okay. If you'll grab our stuff, I'll check around here for flashlights, batteries and whatever else we may need. Then we'll lock up and leave.

"Works for me." Michael inched backwards heading for the bedroom. "They're gonna be okay, Jared. I'm sure of it." He left Jared and rushed to the bedroom.

Throwing clothes and everything else into both of their duffel bags, his stomach churned. Did this have anything to do with the bad feeling he'd had earlier? Michael hoped not.

"Is that it?" Jared asked as Michael emerged from the house.

"I filled the cooler with ice and tossed in some water bottles, but we should probably stock up. The Red Cross may need more."

"Red Cross?" Jared glared at him as though confused.

"We're heading to a disaster area, baby." He skimmed the edge of Jared's hand with his finger. "Are you okay?"

"Yeah, I guess it hasn't sunk in yet."

"I guarantee when we get there, your training will kick in."

"Right." Jared grabbed one of the bags from Michael. "I'll load these into the trunk if you'll get the cooler."

Michael nodded and nudged the second bag in Jared's direction with his foot as he picked up the cooler. "This should fit in the backseat."

"It will."

After they loaded the car, Michael sat in the passenger seat eyeing Jared as he locked the front door and took one last look around the property. Though understandably preoccupied, Jared would probably never show Michael how scared he truly was, and he didn't have to.Michael already saw it.

"Ready?" Jared pulled his seatbelt across his shoulder and fastened it between them.

Michael reached out and squeezed his hand, and they pulled out of the drive leaving the lake-house behind.

****

Traffic was hit and miss, as they drove along Highway 59 headed south. No cars would pass by for miles and miles, and then they'd find themselves literally parked as traffic came to a halt. The final stretch wasn't as busy as Michael expected, but then again, he had no idea what they were about to find when they got to Jared's family's home.

The afternoon sun waned overhead, slowly yielding to nightfall. "Damn. I hoped we'd have more daylight."

"I'm sure they have a search and rescue station set up. They'll have plenty of light for searching at night. Dogs, four wheelers. Hell, EquuSearch is probably already working side by side with the Red Cross."

"Think FEMA has been called in yet?" Bright lights from oncoming cars shone on Jared's face. His eyes were red. Either he was more tired than Michael thought, or he'd been crying.

"I'm sure everyone's there."

Jared didn't comment further, and the car soon became eerily quiet.

As they neared the exit, traffic slowed, and emergency lights flashed ahead.

A roadblock had been set up to reroute traffic. "Mike, hand me your I.D. and EMT credentials."

Michael didn't ask questions. He dug his wallet from his back pocket and handed it over as they came to a stop.

A Harris County Sherriff's Deputy waved them forward and scanned the car with his flashlight.

Jared lowered the window. "Follow my lead."

"Sorry fellas, but we're gonna have to route y'all around the Mission Creek area."

"We understand, officer." Jared displayed both of their I.D.s. "We're medics from Fort Sam. We were on block leave, fishing up near Lufkin, when the storm hit. We thought we may be of assistance."

The officer took both IDs and examined them closely. "Give me a minute, boys. Let me see if I can get y'all in. They can sure use all the help they can get." He clicked the radio mic attached to his shoulder. "Dispatch, this is two-thirty-five down at the Wilson Road redirect. I have two army medics here and need an okay for admittance into Mission Creek."

A female voice replied through the static. "Two-thirty-five, permission granted. All volunteer medical personnel are to report directly to the Red Cross at Fifth and Rosemary."

"Two-thirty-five clear." He handed the wallets back to Jared. "Go through there, and—"

"Take a right onto Main," Jared said. "Thank you, sir. My parents live here. I know exactly where that is."

The officer's eyes widened. "Son, I don't want to alarm you, but things past that last barricade up ahead aren't what they were two days ago. I'm sorry."

Michael eyed Jared as he pressed his lips together and swallowed hard. "Thank you, sir. I understand."

The deputy waved to another man who lifted the first small barricade and signaled for them to pass.

They eased through and drove slowly down the access road, then turned right onto Main. The red-light signals that were supposed to stretch across the intersection dangled from a lone cable.

Twisted street signs either leaned to one side or were completely blown over all along the deserted street. Two billboards on both sides of the road were severely damaged with trash strewn beneath.

"Are you okay?" Michael caressed the back of Jared's hand.

Jared pulled his hand away and gripped the steering wheel. His knuckles flared white, and his jaw ticked. "I should have called before…" He shook his head.

"Don't beat yourself up, Jared. I bet they're fine and helping out." Michael held his breath to calm his own nerves. If only he knew for certain, then whatever they were about to encounter probably wouldn't be so hard to face.

The road soon narrowed, and although it was dark, the headlight beams revealed enough to give them an idea of how bad things would look in the morning. Scattered lumber and tree limbs gave the impression a bomb had detonated.

"Fuck, I haven't seen anything like this since Afghanistan."

Michael's heart skipped a beat, but he chose not to comment. Jared would work this out, and if he needed him, Michael would be there.

A muddy dog trotted along the roadside, his head

hung low, and he looked like he'd been through hell. "Hey, pull over."

"Why?" Jared slowed the car.

"We should take him with us. His owner may be looking for him."

Jared sighed. "Okay, but I wouldn't hold my breath."

The car came to a stop, and Michael grabbed a bottle of water from the cooler, then stepped out of the car. He knelt in front of the vehicle and whistled. "Come here, boy," he called, with a soft but enthusiastic tone.

The dog cowered and approached him cautiously. He had long, shaggy hair, and was not much bigger than a beagle. His cream colored fur was dingy and matted with pieces of briars and twigs. He looked as though he'd been walking for days.

Michael poured a little water onto the pavement to get his attention.

The dog eased up with his shoulders and head lowered, then he glanced up at Michael as if to ask for reassurance.

"Are you thirsty, boy?" Michael poured more water into his cupped hand.

The dog, either past his initial shyness or overcome by thirst, trotted straight to Michael and lapped at the water in his hand.

Michael continued to pour until the entire twenty-ounce bottle had been consumed. "You've had it rough," he said, still using his friendliest tone. He scratched the animal behind the ear, then stood and patted his leg. "Come on. Let's see if we can find your family."

The dog followed behind and jumped into the car along with Michael as if he'd known him forever. He hopped right in the back and peered over the seat at the road ahead.

"Are you happy now?" Jared asked as Michael shut the door.

Michael glanced back at the dog and grinned. "Yes, thank you."

Jared shook his head, put the car in gear and proceeded toward Fifth Street.

As they arrived, cars, trucks and even a few horse trailers were scattered around a huge white tent. Three or four men saddled horses, and a few more checked tires and equipment on the backs of several four-wheelers.

"Search and rescue," Jared mumbled.

"EquuSearch," Michael said.

EquuSearch, a well-known volunteer search team founded by a bereaved Texas father whose teenage daughter had been murdered several years ago, now traveled throughout the southern United States looking for missing persons. Most of the time they searched for missing or lost children and would search until they'd exhausted every resource. With small children missing now, they would have the equipment and man-power to search for days.

"Probably," Jared said.

The surreal moment passed as they parked and left the car. The dog hopped out, but stayed close to Michael.

"Looks like they have a command post in the big tent and triage set up in the smaller one over…" Jared's comment trailed off.

"Why don't you go to the command center and see if they have a list of residents. Maybe your parents have checked in. I'll head over and see if I can help with first aid."

Jared nodded and broke away toward the main tent.

Michael headed for the other tent. "Stay out here,

boy," he said to the dog.

The scruffy animal lay at the entrance and immediately closed his eyes, noticeably worn out.

As Michael entered the opening, he noted a row of cots, filled with injured children and a handful of adults, along one side and three examination tables to the left. Two ladies sat at an intake table, and three more meandered about, checking IVs and updating patients' charts. It was a scene Michael had seen countless times in his line of work.

"May we help you, young man?" A short, older lady who looked to be in her late fifties approached with a clipboard in one hand and a stethoscope draped around her neck.

"No, ma'am. I'm here to help you if I can. I'm an army medic out of Fort Sam." Michael shook her hand.

"Lord, have mercy. We can sure use the extra hands." She eagerly drew him to her and ushered him toward the other lady. "Inez, we have some help."

The other woman, younger, though much heavier, joined them. "Thank you, hon. We're in a holding pattern right now. People are trickling in as they need us, but tomorrow, when the search parties are in full force, it may get crazy."

"Crazy is what I've trained for, ma'am."

Tears welled in her eyes. "Bless you." She squeezed his hand.

A burning lump swelled in Michael's throat at first sight of her emotional display. "It's all going to be okay."

The other lady handed her a tissue, and she wiped her tears. "I'm terribly sorry. It's been a long day, and with everything that's happened in the last twenty-four hours, it's been a bit overwhelming."

"I can only imagine. Tell me where you need me,

and then you can breathe a minute or two."

The other woman sighed. "We've sent the severely injured to the nearest hospitals, and we're waiting for the ambulance to return. With so many areas affected, the Fire Department and EMTs are spread pretty thin. The Red Cross is sending more staff tomorrow, and of course the National Guard is on standby if we need them. We hope to have all these people cleared out as soon as possible."

"How many children are still missing?"

"Six from the daycare, but who knows all together? Some families have been separated, so we've tried our best to reunite them as more victims filter in," the larger woman said.

"My friend's parents live a few blocks from the daycare. We're hoping they're okay."

"Who's your friend, honey?" The older woman asked.

"Jared Prophet."

She nodded. "Jon and Maureen's son. I know the family well."

Michael's stomach sloshed with excitement. "Have you seen them?"

Her expression darkened, and she shook her head. "If they've come through, I haven't seen them."

Michael's gaze dropped to the floor. *Damn.* He'd hoped for better news.

She reached over and patted his arm. "That doesn't mean they aren't fine. Knowing Jon Prophet, he's at home guarding his place like a watch dog."

"I hope so." Michael smiled.

"Why don't you and Jared see if y'all can find them? There will still be plenty of work to do around here when you get back."

"Thank you. Who knows? Maybe he's found

them already."

Michael left them and headed across to the larger tent.

The dog trotted behind him.

"Well?" he asked when he saw Jared coming toward him.

"Nothing. They haven't checked in."

"One of the ladies in the triage tent knows your parents, and she suggested we go over to the house. She's sure they will be there."

"Yeah, I thought the same thing." He stalked toward the car. "You coming?"

"Absolutely." Michael jumped in the passenger seat after the dog crawled into the back.

"Does Sir Muttly have to come, too?"

"Sir Muttly?"

"The dog."

"I guess he does." Michael looked back at the dog. "His name isn't Sir Muttly, though."

"What is it?"

"I don't know. Maybe you should ask."

Jared glared at him and started the car. "Why don't the two of you figure it out and let me know later."

Michael smiled. "We'll do that." Michael had hoped to make Jared smile, but he'd failed. He tried not to make light of the situation or appear as though he didn't care. In truth, Michael probably cared too much.

The drive was very dark, and without the light from streetlamps only the car's headlights illuminated the way.

Jared drove rather slowly, not that he had much of a choice. Trees were down everywhere, and in several places they had to swerve to miss large limbs and other scattered debris.

As they turned onto Jared's parents' street, Jared

stopped the car. "Holy fuck."

Overturned cars and leveled homes lined both sides of the street.

Michael gasped. "Oh my God."

The dog whimpered as though he somehow understood the shock of what they were seeing.

Jared sat there for a moment, then got out and walked in front of the car.

Michael and the dog followed.

"This can't be my street."

Michael reached for him. "Jared—"

"Mom?" Jared took off at a dead run. "Dad!"

Michael barreled after him, not sure exactly where they were going.

Several hundred feet later, Jared came to a halt in front of a giant pile of rubble. Only the partial structure of what appeared to be a garage remained intact.

"No," he growled as he rushed toward what once must have been his home. He climbed over broken boards and twisted aluminum siding. "Dad!" he shouted again.

Michael followed, making his way over upside-down furniture and a shredded mattress with a busted television on top. "Jared, I'm going to get flashlights from the car."

"Hurry," he said. "Try to get the car a little closer."

Michael turned back and ran as fast as his feet could carry him to the car. The dog scampered alongside. He started the car and began to creep through the disastrous remains of the street. His fear grew. What if – what if they were dead? How would Jared handle it? How would either of them handle it? Michael's heart thundered.

Without hesitation, Michael dug his cell phone from his pocket and dialed as he drove.

"Hello?" Joel's voice echoed on the other end of the line.

"Joel." Michael's voice cracked.

"What is it? What happened?"

"The area where Jared's parents live is…shit, Joel, it's fucking gone."

"What?" he exclaimed. "What do you mean *gone*?"

"Tornadoes."

"Fuck. Where are you?"

"An area southeast of Houston called Mission Creek."

"Shit, we saw that on the news." A mumbling sound followed as though Joel had covered the phone, probably relaying information to Alana. "Sit tight. We're on our way."

Michael sighed as relief washed over him. He would need help if the situation turned tragic. "Bring your credentials, and tell them you're from Fort Sam. They should let you in through the roadblock."

"Where are you right now?"

"I'm sitting in front of what used to be their house." Tears stung Michael's eyes as the reality of what might be under the pile of rubble sank into his mind. "The whole neighborhood's wiped out."

"Damn. We're only a couple of hours away."

Michael nodded as if Joel could see him through the phone. "Hurry."

The conversation ended abruptly, and Michael drew in a deep breath, wiped his eyes and popped the trunk. As he opened the back, he heard Jared calling out for his parents, which only added to the angst.

He grabbed two flashlights and headed toward the sound of Jared's voice.

"Jared?"

"Over here."

Michael crawled under a leaning door jamb, amazingly still intact.

Jared straddled another pile of twisted boards in front of Michael. "Wait a second. I think I hear something."

Michael froze, and they listened.

The dog sat beside Michael, and even he closed his mouth. After a few seconds, his furry ears instantly perked up, and then he barked.

Startled by the unexpected eruption, Michael jumped.

"Scratching!" Jared dove back into the pile.

The dog barked again.

Michael joined Jared, and they both pulled boards and what remained of twisted countertops and cabinets from an area of the house that must have been the kitchen.

"Shine the light. I'll dig," Jared said.

Michael turned on both flashlights and pointed the bright beams to where Jared labored.

"Oh, my God. Mom!"

Michael's heart pounded, and Jared reached down and grabbed a frail hand. "Don't try to move, Mom. Let us dig you out."

Michael propped the flashlights against one of the broken cabinets and aided Jared in carefully removing rubble.

"Jared?" she said in little more than a scratchy whisper.

"Be still. Don't move."

Michael squatted as more of her body was revealed. "Mrs. Prophet? We're going to get you out, but it's very important you don't try to move." Michael's medical expertise took hold of his thoughts. He scanned the immediate area around them, searching for anything of use. "Jared, grab that door behind you. We'll need to put her on a flat surface."

Jared looked behind where he stood and made his way to the white door jammed under what looked to have been a microwave. "Got it." He heaved the smashed appliance to the side.

Michael cleared more debris from atop Jared's mother until he was able to take her hand. He reached for her wrist and instinctively checked her pulse. "Good job." He patted the back of her hand. "Nice pulse you have there, ma'am." He glanced up at Jared. "It's strong."

"Mom, you have to be very still. I'm going to move the rest of this stuff, and then we'll move you onto the door to get you out of here."

"Jared?" she said weakly. "Your father?"

Michael inched his way to her as Jared uncovered the rest of her body. "Check her legs. I've got her arms and torso." Michael ran his hands up and down her sides.

Mrs. Prophet winced as his hand pressed down on her ribcage.

Michael smiled down at her. "Looks like you and I have something in common. I have cracked ribs, too." He peered over his shoulder at Jared. "We need something to strap her to this. Maybe some…" He looked around them. "See if you can find some fabric we can tie together."

"Good idea." Jared backed away again. He reached down and grabbed something, then started to pull it from under more debris. "I always hated these drapes."

Michael smiled. Jared had calmed down quite a bit, which was the best thing considering the task at hand. As long as he kept his wits about him, they would be able to move his mother and get her back to the command post much easier.

Jared dug into his pocket and brought out a small pocket knife. "I'll cut them up. Sorry, Mom."

The sound of ripping fabric echoed through the dark.

"Mrs. Prophet, without moving your head, can you verbally tell me if anything else hurts. Any burning or numbness?"

"My…my stomach and back," she said.

"Okay. You probably have some pretty bad bruising. Not surprising considering a house fell on you." He grinned and patted her hand.

A slight smile spread across her face. "Maureen," she faintly whispered.

Michael hadn't heard her clearly. "What's that, ma'am?" He leaned in.

"She wants you to call her Maureen," Jared said.

"It's very nice to meet you, Maureen. I'm Michael." He squeezed her hand. "We're going to get you out of here, now."

"Mom?" Jared spoke up. "Where was dad when the tornadoes hit?"

"He went…" Her brow pinched, and she slightly shook her head. "I think he—" Agitated, she began to struggle. "Jon?"

"Don't worry, Maureen. We'll find him. Take a deep breath, and hold on." Michael glanced over.

Jared's blue eyes watered, and his attention returned to his mother. "Mom, please be very still. Michael and I are gonna move you onto the door. It may hurt, but we're going to be as gentle as we can."

He moved down toward his mother's legs, and Michael positioned himself at her head.

"On three," Michael said. "One…two…"

They lifted her at the same time and eased her onto the door.

Jared wrapped the strips of torn curtain around the door and secured it over her forehead, tying it on the side. He moved down lower toward her middle, jammed his arm under the door and handed the end of another torn strip to Michael, who pulled it out and folded it over her for Jared to tie off. They repeated the step again, securing her all the way down the length of her body.

In a matter of minutes, they'd safely moved her to the sidewalk.

Michael knelt next to Maureen and checked her pulse again. "Jared, go tell search and rescue we found a survivor."

"That's all right, man. I'll stay."

"I have no idea where I am. It will be faster if you go."

Jared looked back and forth between his mom and the car as though contemplating his decision. "You're right."

"Leave me some water. I'm going to do what I do best."

"What's that? Piss me off?"

Michael laughed. "No, I'm gonna flirt with a beautiful lady."

"Mom, if he gets out of line, you have my permission to deck him." Jared bent over and kissed her cheek.

She smiled up at him. "Who said I needed permission?"

Both men laughed as a brief moment of joy settled in the air.

"Maureen, I have a feeling you and I are going to get along great."

Jared rose and gazed down at Michael. "Take good care of my mom."

"I'll treat her as if she were my own."

Jared turned and walked back to the car, giving them one quick glance before he drove away into the night.

Michael then settled beside Maureen and brushed short, blonde curls away from her face. "We'll have you up and around in no time."

"Thank you for helping my son."

He gently caressed her shoulder. "I'd do anything for Jared." And he would.

TYLER ROBBINS

Chapter Twelve

Jared had never been more scared in his life. Not even when he'd been pinned down by a dozen combatants in Afghanistan. He'd kept his cool then and made decisions based on years of training and experience until backup arrived.

But this? This he couldn't have ever prepared for.

How could someone prepare for discovering their mother, alone in the dark, buried by a pile of busted debris that once had been their home?

His mother's injuries weren't life threatening, but his father had yet to be found.

Search and rescue crews spent the remainder of the night looking for Jonathan Prophet under the rubble of their house.

Exhaustion gripped his body, and as badly as he needed rest, he wouldn't stop. He had to know his father was alive.

He leaned against the fire hydrant on the curb, in front of the command center tent watching as crews changed shifts and new volunteers prepared to move out.

Joel and Alana had arrived a couple of hours after he and Michael returned with his mother. Jared never knew Michael had even called them. Though surprised to see April with them, her news of Raul refusing to change his position, hadn't been as unexpected. That bridge had quite possibly been burned, and considering the current disaster, Raul was the least of Jared's worries. His father was his main concern now.

He'd spent so many years filled with anger for his dad. So many years resentful of the man Jared had never been able to please. Staying away was easier than facing him or worse – standing up to him. Now he might never get the chance.

"Are you hungry?" Alana asked as she sat down on the curb beside him.

"Yeah, but I have a feeling if I eat, I'll only throw up."

She leaned her head onto his shoulder. "Your mom's feeling better. Michael hasn't left her side. She's in good hands."

Jared didn't respond. His mind whirled with thoughts of his dad.

"I'm going to find you some coffee and maybe a granola bar. Something light." Alana got to her feet and as she turned to leave him, Jared grabbed her hand.

"Thanks."

"No problem." She squeezed his hand and walked away.

Ready to be a part of the next search party gearing up, Jared got to his feet.

He headed toward the command center, but Michael emerged from the medical tent as he reached the opening.

"How are you?"

The nerve endings at the base of his skull tingled, redirecting his initial intention. He needed Michael's touch more than ever, but as he looked around, he knew it wasn't possible. Not here. Not with so many eyes watching them. "Follow me."

He led the way to an area behind the medical tent where dozens of ATVs and the horse trailers were parked.

"You were amazing with my mother," he said as they stopped between two small trailers.

"I'm glad I was there to help."

Michael gazed at him with those deep chocolate tinted orbs, making Jared's cock ache for his touch. He scanned the area for signs of unwanted prying eyes. "Come here."

Michael inched toward Jared, and the instant he invaded Jared's personal space, Jared grabbed him, shoving his crotch against Michael's hip. He exhaled into Michael's ear, his heart pounding. "God, I need you so fucking bad."

Michael cupped his face and stared deep into Jared's eyes, so deep that a flutter of unrest rippled across Jared's gut.

"I love you, and I'm not going anywhere."

Jared clutched at Michael's shirt as though unable to stand without the other man's help. "You can't love me." He couldn't possibly. It would only make the situation much more difficult and tragic, a complete waste.

"Well, I do."

"Fuck." There was no point in denying it, so why didn't he say it back? He felt the same. He had for days, but the words wouldn't come. "Shut up, and kiss me."

Michael slowly leaned in, and his bottom lip quivered in the morning light, even after his mouth met Jared's. The vibration ricocheted into Jared as though a bolt of electricity had fused them together.

The kiss was deep and passionate, and Jared rubbed against Michael's side, willing himself to come, if only to relieve the tension.

Michael moaned into Jared's mouth. "Five minutes," he whispered. "You need this."

How did Michael know him so well? Five minutes would ease it all. Ease the pain, ease the fear, and ease the uncertainty of everything. Five minutes deep inside Michael and Jared would be capable of handling whatever happened. "Hurry."

Michael tugged at his shirt sleeve. "Over here."

He led Jared down the jumbled row of parked cars to Alana's black Dodge Charger and opened the back door.

Jared perused the parking area for witnesses then ducked inside.

Michael slammed the door closed behind them.

In a heated rush, clothes flew everywhere.

Jared bit and kissed Michael's bare chest as Michael straddled him the way Tiffany had at the strip club. Their cocks rubbed together, and Jared stroked them at the same time with two desperate fists. Michael's prick swelled in Jared's hand causing his balls to tighten and throb.

Forgetting his own, Jared focused on Michael's swollen cock. He thumbed the top, slicking the clear fluid around the head then licking it from his finger. "You're always so fucking sweet."

Michael's breathing became labored as the excitement between them grew. He hunched over to kiss and suckle Jared's neck, while digging his fingers into the flesh of Jared's biceps, squeezing and clenching his arm with desperate need.

Jared jammed his fingers into Michael's mouth, and Michael responded with a delirious roll of his eyes and eagerly sucked them. Jared pulled his fingers back. "Spit," he said.

Michael did as he was told and spat on Jared's fingertips.

Jared reached around Michael's waist and circled his asshole with the tip of his wet fingers, dipping them inside as Michael rocked his ass back and forth, forcing him deeper with each thrust.

Jared grasped the base of his cock and positioned the tip right under Michael's ass. Then Michael eased down onto it until his ass cheeks met Jared's hip bones.

"Fuck." Jared huffed.

Michael rose up, then eased back down, again and again, each time working Jared's cock deeper inside his ass.

Tangled wet tongues warred with one another as Jared gripped Michael's hips and shoved more of himself inside.

Michael groaned into Jared's opened mouth. "Give it to me." Michael grunted.

He clenched his ass cheeks tighter, and Jared gasped, becoming trapped.

"Mike," he whispered between breaths. "I—"

"Now, Jared. Let it go."

Jared fought back the tears that threatened release. His whole body trembled. "I—" He wanted so bad to say it, to tell Michael how he truly felt.

Their bodies rocked back and forth as pressure built in Jared's cock.

Michael grasped his own cock and stroked it faster and faster, keeping pace with the way Jared slammed himself into Michael's ass. He bit his bottom lip and glared down at Jared, sweat beading on his brow.

"I'm gonna—" Jared tried to tell him, but the words caught in his throat as his cock violently pulsed, releasing cum deep into Michael's ass, one glorious blast after another.

Warm spurts of Michael's seed spilled onto Jared's bare chest as their twinned orgasms exploded.

Michael collapsed onto Jared, smearing his cum across both their abdomens.

Jared hugged him hard and buried his face into the curve of Michael's neck. He kissed him there and held him close.

Michael eventually pulled away and spayed his fingers through Jared's wet hair. He toyed with it, slicking it back. "Feel better?"

Jared lifted his chin to meet Michael lips with his. The tender kiss didn't come close to conveying the way he felt about the other man, and words were of no use. He kissed him again before taking note of the steamed windows.

"Guess we got a little carried away? We forgot a condom again."

Michael laughed. "Making love to you, it's impossible not to get carried away, and I'm not worried about the condom. We're tested all the time, so don't worry."

Jared stared at Michael's beautifully chiseled face and skimmed his fingers across his hard chest. "Thank you for being here for me."

Michael cupped Jared's face in his hands. "Like I said, I'm not going anywhere."

Jared believed that. If he'd never believed anything before, he damn sure trusted that. "We *do* need to go somewhere, and that's back to the real world."

Michael rose up and eased Jared's spent cock from his ass causing Jared to wince as it flopped onto his thigh. Michael chuckled again. "Sorry, baby."

Jared grinned. "It's okay. It was worth it."

They fumbled around in the car and managed to put their clothes back on. "I'll go first." Michael leaned over and kissed him.

Jared sat in the backseat as Michael left the car. He waited a few seconds for Michael to step away, and then he emerged behind him and looked around for other people.

Emotions ran wild especially as Jared struggled to form the words he needed so badly to say to Michael. He owed the other man that much.

"Mike." He reached for him. Then, remembering where they were, he let his hand drop to his side, unsatisfied. His throat burned, and his heart pounded relentlessly. "I have to tell you something."

Michael inched toward him, his brow bent with noticeable concern. "What is it?"

Jared shivered and he gulped away a heated ball of air constricting his throat. Tears stung his eyes once again, and that vulnerable, tender place, he'd never allowed himself to reveal, rushed toward the surface of his heart. But instead of the words he needed to say, Jared succumbed to the pain and cried.

Michael pulled him close and caressed the back of his head. "Jared, it's okay. You don't have—"

Jared inhaled, gathering the strength he needed. "No. I have to say this."

He clutched Michael's shirt collar and moved so close to Michael's face he felt the warm exhalations emanating from Michael's nose. "I should have told you days ago," Jared said. "But I let pride or plain ol' stubbornness keep me from it." Jared jerked at Michael's twisted collar as the words danced on his tongue, begging for release. "I—"

"Jared?"

Jared instantly released Michael and shoved him back as a commanding voice he knew all too well spoke sharply behind them.

He whirled around the see where the sound had come from. Had he imagined it?

Jared's body became rigid as the familiar image of his father began to take shape and stepped into view from behind one of the horse trailers.

"Dad?" Jared stood there, shock seizing every muscle of his body.

"Mr. Prophet," Michael said, his voice chipping away at the dizzying swirl confusing Jared's overwrought mind.

Jared watched as Michael rushed toward his father, catching him as his knees buckled beneath him. His tattered clothes were covered in mud and dirt, his hair, a disheveled grey mess, swirled atop his head. Deep wrinkles plowed across a ruddy, over exposed complexion.

He was alive. Alive, and all too aware of the forbidden intimacy between Jared and Michael.

Jared's first instinct was to run and hide, cower in the corner, far from view of the disappointment he knew he'd find in his father's eyes.

"Jared, help me." Michael lifted Jared's father from under his arms.

In a heartbeat of recognition, Jared's mind slammed back to reality. "I've got him," he said as he took over for Michael and leaned his dad against the tire well of the horse trailer behind him. "Go get help."

Michael left and disappeared around the back of the horse trailer.

Jared propped his dad up and lifted his eyelids to inspect his pupils. He gently gripped his wrist and checked his pulse. "Dad, can you hear me?"

Stone cold, black eyes glared back at him. His jaw ticked, and a scowl Jared hadn't seen since he was a child, contorted his father's face. "Never tell you mother. It will kill her."

"Dad – I…" words escaped him. Shame as intense as the humiliation he'd felt when he was twelve, infiltrated Jared's gut, and he covered his lips to prevent the sickening swill churning in his gut from spewing from his mouth.

"Mr. Prophet…" the sound of one of the nurses echoed from behind them.

Jared's world spun out of control as though he were trapped in some horrible nightmare with no hope of waking.

Several more people came to help.

The moment the rescue workers took his father away, Jared collapsed onto his knees and purged his body of the vile disgust that inhabited his body. He vomited until the back of his throat blazed with a stinging fire, and he tasted blood. Even then he prayed more repugnance would be regurgitated until all of the feelings he'd held for Michael were expelled. Dispersed back into the abyss right where they should have stayed.

Michael's scent permeated around him. His taste still lingered on Jared's tongue. Jared rose and stumbled to the back of the horse trailer, barely able to stand, wishing it had been him who'd been ripped from the earth by the tornadoes instead of homes and those poor innocent children.

He should be punished, not them, not those good people, and certainly not the kids.

"Jared?" Alana's voice called out.

Jared winced when her hand touched his shoulder.

"Your mother is asking for you."

Jared waved her off, unable to look her in the eyes.

"Jared!" She rushed to his side.

"Leave me, please?" He turned away, intent on avoiding as much of her as possible.

"Your dad's going to be okay, but your mom asked me to find you."

"Why?" What did she want? A normal son? One who would give her grandchildren? A son worth bragging about to her friends at church? "What does she want?"

Alana stepped back. "I…Jared, are you okay?"

"I'm fine." He stood upright and squared his shoulders.

"O-okay." Something in her shaky tone told him

she didn't believe him.

He'd have to convince her. "Tell her I'm a little overwhelmed, but I'll be right there." It wasn't exactly a lie.

"All right." She backed away and left.

He'd avoided eye contact, and luckily, she hadn't pressed further. *What a relief.* Jared drew in a deep breath and wiped his mouth.

Once again, Michael's scent wafted into his nostrils. He charged to the medical supply cabinet at the entrance of the tent and pulled out a bottle of alcohol then poured it into his hands, ridding his skin of any trace of Michael Crest. If only he were able to bathe in it, then he'd remove Michael from every pore of his body.

Jared meandered through the crowd gathered around his father and zeroed in on the cot where his mother lay resting.

His peripheral vision, though deliberately clouded, detected the outline of Michael to her left, but Jared kept his eyes set on her. If he looked at Michael now, he'd probably kill him with his bare hands to stop the pain. Fuck Michael for turning his life upside-down. Fuck his charming personality and those *"fuck me"* bedroom eyes. Fuck everything about the man that had ever captured Jared's attention.

"Jared," his mom spoke with a weakened voice. She reached for him. "They say your father is fine. Dehydrated and a little disoriented, but he'll he okay."

"That's good, Mom." He brought her hand to his mouth and kissed the back of her fingers.

"Promise me you won't leave until they find those missing children."

"Mom, you need to worry about you and dad, and the search team will handle the missing kids."

"No!" She squeezed his hand firmly. "You,

Michael and your friends have to help. They need your expertise. They need your medical training."

"There are plenty of trained professionals here, Mom. My concern is you and Dad."

"Don't argue with me. Now you and Michael do what you do best and…" Her voice trailed off as she moved her free hand away.

Jared held his breath as his mother took Michael's hand and drew it back to where she held Jared's. She then placed Michael's hand on top of his.

Jared flinched.

"The two of you are a team, and you need to work together and bring those babies home. Promise me."

"I promise, Maureen," Michael said.

Jared swallowed hard, struggling to remain calm. Touching Michael's hand became too much to take. He quickly slid his out from under the pile without even glancing in Michael's direction. "Yes, ma'am." Jared turned on his heel and left the tent.

The second the sun shone on his face Jared regained his composure in the hot summer heat and set his mind to the task at hand. He'd do what his mother asked. He'd honor her wishes and make her proud, and if that meant sticking around to find the missing children, he'd do it. He'd do whatever it took to redeem himself in her eyes and even his father's eyes. Somehow, some way, he'd be the son they needed him to be.

Jared headed straight to where the searchers gathered on the other side of the command center tent.

People stood around talking, and a few checked fanny packs for whatever supplies they'd planned to carry with them. Jared needed none of that. He only required a map of the areas to be searched, his cell phone and some water. He damn sure didn't need wet wipes or hand sanitizer. What were these people planning for, a rescue or a picnic?

"We really don't have time for this bullshit." He looked around, his fingers twitching to take action.

The entire neighborhood was demolished, and there seemed no end in sight to the twisted metal and random, out of place debris. A dented refrigerator still lay in the middle of the street, and off to the side of where they'd gathered, a mangled tricycle reminded him that more than material things had been lost in the storm.

According to the latest news, none of the six children from the daycare had been found from the night search. Of course, a large number of people had been diverted to Jared's house to dig for his dad. His dad, who had walked up from out of nowhere as though he'd been out for an early morning stroll rather than swept away by a killer tornado in the middle of a tropical storm.

Precious time had been wasted. Time they couldn't get back.

What is the hold-up? Why doesn't someone insist they hurry? His nerves were stretched to the limit. Jared had to move. He had to be out there scouring the forest, digging through debris – anything that would guarantee distance between him and Michael. His stomach churned. Could the missing children fare as well as his father? It had been nearly forty-eight hours already. Would they be able to hold out much longer?

Jared's composure inched closer to unraveling, right as the sheriff rushed up to address the four dozen or so men and women who'd volunteered for the God-forsaken task.

"Thank you, all," the sherriff said.

Finally.

A flutter of movement signaled the change of atmosphere at the thought of whatever news he had brought.

"Just got word that four of the six missing children have been found and are being air lifted to Texas Children's Hospital as we speak."

Whoops and hollers erupted from the group.

"Now before you get too excited, none of the children were found anywhere near the daycare. In fact, two were found four blocks away and the other two farther than that. This means our search grid has been expanded, and time is of the essence." He reached over to another officer and took something from him. "We will be dividing everyone up into sections according to color. Canvass the areas as we've been doing. Make sure you freeze in place if you hear a whistle. One will be sounded in the event someone hears something such as a whimper or a cry. Any sounds from one of the kids will probably be faint, so don't expect them to be screaming. They're tired, hungry, thirsty and you can bet, their scared to death. They may even be injured. So be prepared for anything. Any questions?"

A woman at the front of the group raised her hand. "Which kids are still out there?"

"Cousins, Sabrina Knowles and Shane Price. Shane is six, and Sabrina is four." He held up flyers with the children's photos and information. "These are available along with the maps. Any other questions?"

The sheriff scanned the crowd. "Okay, let's go find our kids."

"I have your maps and flyers. Each map has different areas cordoned off, so only search in the highlighted area of your map. Stay together. Leave no stone unturned," a deputy shouted as he handed out the information.

Jared waited his turn and grabbed a map and flyer. After examining the map, he rushed off toward the southeast side of the neighborhood, the side where an old dried up creek bed ran down between two steep embankments.

He hadn't been there in years, but he remembered it all too well as the spot where he and his friends jumped homemade ramps on their bicycles there when they were kids. Back when the world was safe and he was still innocent. Back before all hell had broken loose and he'd been worth saving. Long before anyone like Michel Crest had ever entered his mind.

Chapter Thirteen

The bad feeling Michael often had – the foreboding one, the same feeling that had plagued Michael since the day he and Jared shared a smoke in the bathroom at the base – had returned.

Something was up. Something Michael had missed. Hard to believe though, considering they'd relieved their *"stress"* in each other's arms less than half an hour ago.

Jared hadn't even acknowledged Michael when he came inside to see his mother. In fact, Jared acted as though Michael hadn't existed at all. But why? Why would he do something like that, especially when he'd been so close to sharing his feelings? Michael didn't know for sure, but with the way Jared looked into his eyes and held him so fiercely, he felt Jared was about to make a declaration. A declaration not unlike the one Michael had already made.

"Excuse me, Maureen," Michael said with a caring smile. "I'm going to check in and see if they need us elsewhere."

"April and I will stay here. You two find Jared and join a search team," Alana said.

Joel excused himself, as well, and they left the girls to care for Jared's mom.

As they exited the tent, the scruffy dog immediately trotted over and sat at Michael's feet.

"Friend of yours?" Joel asked.

"Something like that."

Joel bent down and gave the animal a rub behind the ears. "So what's up with Jared?"

Michael peered down at his friend. "Not sure exactly, but if I had to guess, I'd say there's a strong possibility his father said something to him. We were kind of in the middle of something when he wandered up."

Joel groaned then stood back up. "Say it ain't so. We are *literally* in the middle of a disaster area, and you two still had to hook up and in broad daylight?"

"He was stressed, and I tried to help."

"Stressed or not, people can't go around humpin' like rabbits every time the mood strikes."

Michael folded his arms across his chest. "Oh, like you're not all over Alana every chance you get?"

"All right, all right, I get your point." Joel looked around as if scouting the area then leaned in and spoke in a hushed tone, "Um, if Alana and I happened to need a little stress relieving, where would we find some privacy around here?"

Michael laughed as he strolled away. "Try the backseat of her car." He glanced back over his shoulder awaiting Joel's response.

"Awe, man. I'm sorry I asked."

Michael stopped and waited for Joel to catch up. "Stop thinking about sex, and let's find Jared." Their personal lives would wait. Missing kids couldn't. "Remember why we're here."

"Sorry, man." Joel nodded, and his expression adopted a more somber air. "It looks like everyone is gathered over on the other side of the command center tent. Maybe they've set up the next search team."

As they approached, Michael thought he saw Jared walking toward the parking area. Surely Jared hadn't left without him. "Do you see him?"

Joel shook his head. "Hey, grab a map from that deputy."

Michael approached the tall, gangly officer who didn't look old enough to be out of high school. The map he handed him had orange markings in the lower left hand corner. "This is our search area?"

The deputy glanced at the map. "Yes, and that creek bed is dry, but it's steep. You definitely want to watch your step. There's no telling what the tornadoes dumped in there."

Michael noted the patterns and recognized the symbols in the legend box. "Wait, is this an old well or water main in this section?"

The deputy leaned in and looked closer. "Hold on a minute, and let me check this."

Michael released the map and waited with Joel as the deputy spoke to an older man with a deep receding hairline. The older gentleman moved his finger back and forth over the area in orange and nodded a bunch as he spoke.

"Thanks." The deputy shook the man's hand and returned to Michael and Joel. "The surveyor said in the original plans, the developers intended the subdivision to be part of a self-sustaining community with its own Municipal Utility District, but the plans were scratched a few years later when the city initiated its own plan to provide sewer and water to the outlying communities. They kept the lines and water tower up, but that came down in Hurricane Alicia in eighty-three. My dad told me about it growing up, but I never knew where it was."

"Humph, okay. We'll check it out."

"Good luck, and thanks so much for helping."

"No problem. I hope we find them soon."

"From your lips to God's ears."

Michael and Joel walked to the parking lot where several groups gathered around trucks and ATVs.

"Look for people with orange colored markings," Michael told Joel.

"Over there." Joel pointed toward a white Ford F150 pickup truck. "Hey, can we catch a ride with y'all?"

They jumped in the back of the truck with a few other volunteers, followed by the dog. They were on their way within a couple of minutes.

Michael searched the crowds for Jared as they passed other groups. Where in the hell had he gone, and why hadn't he waited?

Michael tried not to worry too much about unimportant things, but Jared wasn't exactly unimportant anymore. If anything, he was too important.

The streets were littered with debris, scraps really, broken pieces of what had once been homes and possessions of the people who'd lived there. Most of the homes were completely leveled, but then came the occasional house on every block, eerily standing alone, untouched, as though transported from another time and place after the devastation.

Tornadoes were curious beasts. One moment, the weather phenomena appeared to destroy everything within reach, but then in the next it became picky, plucking what it wanted, as though choosing fruit from a stand at a farmers' market. Taking with it only what it chose and leaving the rest behind.

They approached the isolated search area, positioned at the back of the neighborhood. The location made perfect sense considering they had intended it to be the hub of a self-sustaining utility district.

The stray dog followed Michael and Joel as they fanned out in a line along with the other volunteers. Each took their time, searching closely, examining anything that looked out of place or peculiar, which under the circumstances, included pretty much everything.

By the time they reached what remained of the water tower, most of the other searchers had stopped for water breaks or advanced toward the creek bed. The hot sun pelted down relentlessly, but Michael and Joel were used to the heat. Hell, they had no choice. If they couldn't handle Texas heat, how would they survive the desert? The Middle East promised to be a hell-hole.

A tall cyclone fence surrounded a small concrete building and a huge rusted tank. Large white pipes, anywhere from twelve to thirty-six inches in diameter or even more, jutted up from the ground then bent at ninety degree angles, bolted together at six-foot intervals. Several valves and gauges clustered along the line gave the impression the facility might have been in service, with the exception of the rusty, gaping hole in the side of the huge holding tank.

"Do you think we should look in there?" Joel bent his fingers through the squares of the chain-link fence as he peered inside.

"I don't know. Do you see a break in the fence where a kid might squeeze through?"

"Not on this side." Joel narrowed his gaze as he stared across the fenced in area. "Better make a sweep around to the other side."

"Good idea. I'll go left. You circle around to the right, and we'll meet on the other side."

Joel nodded and took off down the fence line.

Michael headed in the opposite direction and scanned the fence up and down looking for a break. The entire site wasn't any larger than an acre or so, but he carefully checked every inch to be sure.

The dog stayed close by his side, though Michael hardly noticed him anymore.

As they reached the far corner, Michael stopped. A section of the fence was peeled back, as though intentionally gapped open enough for someone to crawl through.

He surveyed the property on the other side and noticed a couple of five gallon buckets turned upside down behind the small, grey, brick building. Between the buckets appeared what may have been the remnants of a campfire.

"What do you think, boy? Squatters?" Michael didn't wait for a response from his furry companion. He crawled under the fence and went to see for himself.

Under one of the buckets, Michael found an old coffee can. The second he opened it, he recognized the scent. "I guess some of the local kids come here to get high." *Insane.* Two-story homes had been obliterated by the storm, but some kid's weed stash was still safe and dry under a plastic bucket. *Damn.*

Michael opened the Ziploc baggie and sprinkled the marijuana onto the ground, then rubbed it into the dirt with his boot. "If Jared's parents can't have their house, then these twerps can't have their weed," he said to the dog.

The dog sniffed the ground then sat back on his haunches with his tongue hanging out and looked up at Michael as though awaiting instructions.

"What did you find?" Joel's voice reverberated against the building.

"About ten dollars' worth of weed." Michael chuckled and shook his head.

"Shit, and we can't even smoke it."

"Nope." He sighed. "Well, since we're here, we may as well have a look around."

They continued toward the middle of the water plant. "That's a huge hole in that tank. Big enough for a small kid to fit through, wouldn't you say?"

Joel nodded. "If I was six and scared shitless, I'd probably want to hide."

They made their way through the twisted pipes.

"What did you find?" Jared's voice sounded behind them.

Michael whirled around, shocked at his sudden appearance. "You scared the shit out of me."

The dog left Michael's side and scampered toward Jared, meeting him halfway as he stalked toward them. "The creek bed was a bust. There weren't even any trees down."

"Well, this may be a waste of time, too, but we thought we'd give it a shot," Michael said.

Joel ducked under a pipe that stretched from the small building to the side if the tank. "That holding tank doesn't look stable."

Jared didn't even look in Michael's direction. "Nope." He followed behind Joel.

Seriously? What the hell is wrong with him?

Joel approached the hole in the side of the tank.

Jared eased up behind him, and together they ducked their heads inside.

"Shane?" Jared called out.

"Son of a bitch." Joel's voice reverberated off the inside walls.

Jared suddenly stepped back and scanned the upper area of the tank.

"What is it?" Michael's heart skipped a beat.

"We see him!" Joel shouted.

"How the hell did he get in there?" Jared paced back and forth, still eyeing the top of the tank. "Did he crawl through that hole then fall?"

Michael rushed to the hole and peered over into the tank.

A small child huddled on the far side opposite the busted hole about ten feet below where they stood.

"I don't think the bottom is solid," Michael shouted, glancing over his shoulder. Where the hell had Jared gone this time?

"Shane?" Joel called out again.

The boy didn't respond.

Michael swallowed hard. "That's not good." He moved back and looked around for Jared.

After a few seconds, movement above his head caught his attention.

"Jared? What are you doing?"

Jared peered down at Joel and Michael from atop the tank. "Call for help. Tell them we'll have to be lowered down to get him."

Joel grabbed his cell phone and made the call.

"Jared, are there any rungs on the inside so we can climb down to him until they get here?"

Jared stared down at him. "They're rusted. I don't think they'll hold me."

Michael headed to the other side of the tank where he found the outer rungs Jared must have used to climb to the top. He scaled the side without a second thought. As he reached the surface, he saw for several blocks. From the air, the devastation was overwhelming. The only things remaining in the entire subdivision were a few trees and the occasional untouched home. "Son-of-a-bitch."

"You shouldn't be up here."

"I'm an EMT. If anyone should climb down, it's one of us. I'm smaller, so maybe the rungs will hold me."

"Fuck if you will." Jared's brow furrowed deep.

Michael shook his head in disbelief. "Are you telling me I can't go?" *This should be good.*

Jared's demeanor instantly changed. He raised his hands as if to back down. "Whatever. It's your neck."

Once again, his behavior conflicted. One minute hot, the next, cold as ice.

Michael headed to a square hatch in the roof.

"Help's on the way," Joel shouted.

Michael raised the hatch and scanned the inner

walls. The only way to know would be to do it. He lowered himself through the hatch and reached for the top rung. As soon as he had a firm grip he let go of the hatch rim and began to climb down the rectangular rungs attached to the inside of the tank.

A slight scratching sound echoed from inside the dark tank, followed by what must have been sobbing. "Hey, Shane," he said as kindly as possible. "I'm Michael, and I'm coming to help you."

He'd hoped for a response, but wasn't surprised not to get one. "It's been a couple of scary days, huh, buddy?"

As Michael became even with the gaping hole about four feet over from where the rings descended, Joel stuck his head inside. "I see him, but he isn't moving."

"Shane?" Michael tried again. "Can you hear me?"

The two men shared a worried look. Then Michael continued on. When Shane was in clear view, Michael looked up to see Jared peering down through the hatch at the top of the tank. Even in the dark, Michael noted the concern in Jared's expression.

Michael stepped down on the next rung, but as his full weight settled on the corroded steel, it gave way; and without warning Michael slipped, plummeting about six feet onto the ledge from Shane's huddled little body.

He hit the surface with a violent thud, knocking his breath away. "Crap." Pain stabbed his side.

"Are you okay?" Joel asked.

Michael sat up, leaned against the side wall and gathered his senses, fighting through the pain. "Yeah, but if I do that one more time, what's left of my ribs will be pulverized to dust."

He glanced back up to the top of the tank just as Jared's darkened silhouette disappeared from view.

Michael shrugged it off and focused on Shane who, while only a few feet away, seemed even smaller now. "Hey, Shane." He inched toward him, mindful of every move he made.

Crawling across in the dark, Michael nearly fell again when his hand went through the rusted steel floor. "Hey, guys, bad news."

"What?" Joel replied.

"This isn't the bottom. It's sort of a shelf that goes around the outer edge."

"Can you see the bottom?"

Michael leaned over the side into total darkness. He searched the floor around him for something to toss down and found a rock about the size of a golf ball. Michael grabbed it and dropped it over into the dark. After a few seconds, he heard a slight splash. "I hear water, but I can't tell how deep or how far down."

"Let's not find out. Get the kid, and get the hell out of there."

Joel's impatient tone didn't help Michael's already tattered nerves. "Okay, don't get your panties in a wad. I'm trying."

Michael crawled on all fours toward the boy. "Shane, can you hear me?"

Slowly, the boy raised his head and looked up at him with tear-stained eyes.

"I need to make sure you're all right before we move you, okay, buddy?"

Shane responded with a slight nod.

"Does it hurt anywhere?"

"Y-yes," he said with a scratchy voice.

Michael lifted Shane's head and checked his pupils, ears and head. "Where does it hurt?"

"My arm."

"Okay, well we'll take a look at that in a minute."

Michael glanced around. How much movement would it take to cause the deteriorated ledge to give way? Moving him too much wasn't a good idea. "Shane, I'm gonna reposition you very carefully, so I can get a better look at your arm and the rest of you. Is that okay?"

Shane sniffled and nodded.

"Joel, where's that back-up we asked for?"

"They're here," Joel yelled down.

Michael looked back over his shoulder. "Tell them I'll need a rescue basket and a saline drip."

"Will do."

Michael slowly brought Shane's tiny body toward him and laid him back onto the ledge. "Does this hurt?" He gently moved his hands down the child's right arm.

Shane winced.

"Okay, I'm sorry for that." He mussed the boy's golden hair. Big blue eyes peered up at him, full of fear. He'd seen that look before, only on a much larger version of a scared little boy. Jared.

"You know, you remind me of a good friend of mine. He was a brave kid like you when he was your age, and you know what?"

"What?"

"He grew up to be a big, strong man, and he's a soldier in the Army like me. In fact, he's the bravest soldier I know, and someday, maybe you'll grow to be like him."

"You're a soldier?"

"I am."

"Do you shoot people?"

Michael chuckled. *Why do they always ask that?* "No, buddy, I fix people who are sick or hurt."

"Like a doctor?"

"Sometimes, but mostly it's like the guys you see in ambulances."

A pleased smile stretched across the boy's face. "That's what I wanna be."

"That's great. The Army needs more brave guys like you."

"Michael?" Joel stuck his head back through the hole. "They're lowering the basket stretcher through the hatch, but we've decided it would be best for you to guide it up the rungs then swing him over to me. We can pull him through the hole safer than hauling him to the top. They'd have to cut that open, and we don't have time for that."

"Understood." Michael returned his attention to Shane. "You ready, soldier?"

"Yes." He nodded his head just a bit.

Michael grabbed the basket as it reached them and scooted it beside Shane. It was a tight squeeze, but the six-year old was small; and Michael lifted him with ease, then strapped him in.

"I need to put an IV in your arm, and I'm not gonna lie, dude. It's gonna pinch a bit. Okay?"

Shane's eyes pooled with tears.

"Soldiers have to do stuff like this all the time," Michael spoke softly while he inserted the needle. "But we know we're helping those who can't help themselves. A true soldier protects with honor and courage. I know you're gonna make a great one."

Shane nodded as he looked up at Michael. His bottom lip quivered, and he bit down on it as if to put on a brave face.

"Guess what?" Michael asked.

"What?"

"It's done, and you didn't even flinch."

Shane's big blue eyes widened, and a grin returned to his dirty face.

"We're ready," Michael shouted and got to his

feet. The basket began to rise, and Michael held it tight as he climbed the rungs.

When he reached the level of the hole, Joel yelled for them to stop.

Michael pushed as Joel leaned inside and grabbed the basket from him. Then Joel dragged the basket and Shane through the hole, disappearing into the bright sunlight outside.

Michael made his way to the top and back down to the ground where he met several rescue workers who clapped and patted him on the back.

"Any luck with the girl?"

One of the paramedics glanced up at him from where he knelt next to Shane and the basket. "We're still looking."

Michael squatted beside them. "Shane, did you see your little cousin after the storm?"

Shane nodded. "It was raining, so I crawled through the hole and fell. She ran away."

"Thanks, buddy." Michael stood.

"Well at least we know she was in this area after the storm," Joel said. "That should be good news."

Michael scanned the area, looking past the dispersing crowd that had gathered. Where had Jared gone?

"If you're looking for Jared, he went that way." Joel knew Michael all too well. "I'm going back with the kid. Will you be okay out here?"

"Yeah, man, I'm good. I'm gonna keep looking."

Most of the crowd wandered away as soon as the ambulance pulled out. Joel hopped into the front with the driver and waved as they left.

Michael took a deep breath and looked around for Jared once again. The little girl was still missing, and Jared would most likely want to keep searching if he knew.

"There you are," he said as he approached Jared near a thicket of trees. "The boy's gonna be okay, but the little girl is still out here. Shane said she ran away when he fell through the hole."

Jared continued walking toward the edge of the woods near the creek bed.

"Did you hear me?" Michael quickened his pace. "Jared, stop." He reached for his arm.

Jared whirled around with his fist drawn back as though ready to punch Michael in the face.

"What the hell is wrong?" Michael jumped back. "Were you really gonna hit me?"

Even angry, Jared was still the sexiest man Michael had ever laid eyes on. Though shocked by the reaction, Michael found himself somewhat aroused by his lover's brooding behavior. He took a chance and stepped closer. His need to reconcile became his top priority.

Jared shoved Michael against a tree and clenched Michael's jaw in his left hand and squeezed. Every ounce of his body language screamed domination.

Michael gasped, his heart thundering in his chest. Maybe Jared's frustration had gotten the better of him again. Would he actually initiate a passionate exchange? Right out there in the open?

Jared's jaw flexed rigid, instantly causing Michael's cock to swell. He searched Jared's blue eyes for a clue, even a hint, as to what was truly on his mind. How could he stand so close and not kiss him? Couldn't Jared feel Michael's erection throbbing against his leg?

Hot breath poured over Michael's cheek as Jared held him there, pinned against the tree.

"Jared?" Michael managed to ask. He swallowed hard, trying to catch his breath.

"Leave me the fuck alone. Don't talk to me, don't

even look at me." Jared's blue eyes darkened. "I want you to go. Go home. Go with Joel. I don't care. Go anywhere as long as it's not here."

What the fuck? Is he serious? Michael held his breath to prevent Jared's rugged scent of aftershave mixed with dirt and sweat from engulfing his remaining senses. Confusion didn't come close to describing the whirlwind of emotions brewing inside Michael's mind. "I don't understand."

Jared's smoldering gaze gave the impression of deep passion, begging release, but behind it, a darker intent lurked as though preparing to claw its way to the surface to ruin everything Michael had ever dreamed of.

What should he do? Allow his lips to skim over Jared's and unleash the passionate hunger, or should he run like hell to avoid the sting of the other beast hiding in the dark?

A kiss might free Jared of his evident anguish, but releasing whatever else resided there, felt ominous and wrong. "Okay."

Jared released Michael and stared at the ground between them. His shoulders deflated.

Had backing-off been enough to bring him back from the edge?

"Let me do what I need to do – alone. That's all I'm asking."

Scared to death of losing him, Michael eyed Jared up and down then jammed his hands down into his jean's pockets to keep from reaching out.

No matter how badly he wished Jared didn't mean it, if Michael pushed too hard, Jared would either kill him on the spot or slam him to the ground and fuck the hell out of him. And as much as he'd prefer the latter, the risk was too much. Besides, if Jared needed to get past whatever tormented him, he would need to do it on his own.

"Fine. I'm gone." Michael turned on his heel and headed past a pile of rubble lodged between two mangled trees. If he didn't get away, he'd mess everything up for sure.

He didn't look back, not even to check if Jared had watched him leave.

The farther away he got though, the angrier he became. He'd done everything possible to be there for Jared, and this was the thanks he got? It didn't make any sense, and it damn sure wasn't fair.

"Fuck him." He stomped through the debris back toward the command center. Michael kicked at the ground, and then without even thinking about it, he slammed his fist into what once had been a garage door, or at least that's what the twisted sheet of metal resembled.

Pain bolted across his knuckles followed by a searing fire. The metallic scent of blood flooded his nostrils, and he knew in an instant he'd gone too far. "Shit!"

Michael gave up and leaned against a small tree then slid to the ground. The back of his throat burned as he fought back the flood of tears that threatened to breach. He swallowed hard and drew his knees up to his chest.

The pain of his hand faded as another pain, a deeper pain rushed to the surface. He'd fallen in love with yet another guy who couldn't be himself. Jared had to have loved him. Michael knew it with all his heart. But once again, Michael had given his heart to someone who didn't love him enough to admit it or enough to fight for the possibility of a future together.

Fuck him. Hell, fuck 'em all.

BEYOND HONOR

TYLER ROBBINS

Chapter Fourteen

Jared wandered through the creek bed, making his way over every inch of ground within the orange coded grid. The missing little girl was nowhere to be seen. Jared's legs ached, and his heart hurt even more.

If only he could man up and do what needed to be done. If only he would face his fears and fight the demons that twisted his insides with the destruction of a meat grinder. If only his father were capable of seeing he had a good son. If only. *If only.*

He made his way back to his car and returned to the command center. The volunteers were busy packing up medical supplies and loading boxes into a Red Cross van.

His heart sank. Alana's black Dodge Charger had gone.

Michael had left after all, like Jared had ordered him to do. He sat behind the wheel for a moment, fatigue weighing heavy on his shoulders. Or was it the weight of guilt from being so cruel to a man he knew truly loved him? He'd probably never know, and it didn't matter anyway. What's done was done.

Jared left the car and made his way to the triage tent.

He approached a short, older woman who scribbled on a clipboard. "Excuse me, my parents were here earlier. Do you know where they are?"

"All the patients were moved to the hospital after they found the last two children."

His heart leapt with joy. "They found the little girl, too?"

"Honey, that little angel was in God's hands for sure. She walked out of the woods like nothing had ever happened, asking for her mom and an apple juice box."

Jared drew in a deep breath to force away the surge of emotions that threatened to overwhelm him. "Thank you."

He turned to walk away, but as he did, another woman called out. "Hey, are you Maureen Prophet's boy?"

Jared stopped. "Yes, ma'am. I am."

"She told me to tell you that she and your dad are at Calvary Memorial and for you to make sure that dog gets a good home."

"Dog?" Jared had forgotten all about the dog.

"It should be right out there. It's been around here all evening."

"Thanks." Jared went outside and found the stray dog right where she said he would, asleep beside the tent. "What am I supposed to do with you?"

The dog opened his eyes and arched one brow as if to reply.

"Well, come on. I'm sure they'll have some idea at the hospital."

He and the dog got into his car and drove away. Jared glanced up into the rearview mirror, thinking of the total devastation he'd left behind. More than homes and property had been annihilated in the last couple of days. His life had become one of the casualties, and he only had himself to blame.

****

The hospital bustled with throngs of people. Media vans littered the parking lot, and people rushed around like worker ants rebuilding a colony.

"Stay here, boy," Jared told the dog as he rolled down the windows.

The dog lifted his head and looked up at him, then lay back down and closed his eyes.

"Humph." *Easy enough.*

Jared hurried inside to find his parents. According to the patient information desk, his mom had been taken to the fifth floor, room five-thirty-one.

He silently rode the elevator, uninterested in the other people around him.

As he entered his mother's room, he found her sitting upright in a bed. For the first time he had a chance to see her in bright light. His stomach swam with nausea when the bruises on her frail body became more evident.

"Oh, Mom." He sighed as he sat on the edge of her bed.

She smiled and patted his hand. "This is nothing."

"I'm so thankful you and Dad are okay." He glanced around the room. "Where is he?"

"He's on the phone with your uncle in the waiting room."

"Awe, man. I forgot to call and let him know you were both safe."

"Well, you've been busy."

Jared caressed the back of her hand, careful not to press too hard. "How long are they keeping you here?"

"The doctor says I have two cracked ribs, but I should be able to leave tomorrow."

"Where will you and dad go? Is FEMA coming with relief?"

"We're not waiting for FEMA. Your uncle is already contacting the insurance company and will have adjusters ready by the time we get there."

The nerves on the nape of Jared's neck tingled. "Get there?"

"Florida."

"What do you mean?"

His mother took his hand in hers. "Son, there's nothing left here anymore. The house is gone, and rebuilding is out of the question. Your aunt and uncle love retirement, and your father and I will be able to enjoy ours even more if we're all together."

Jared stood, his heart breaking all over again. "What about me? I'm here."

Her sweet smile warmed him all over exactly as it had when he suffered from nightmares as a small boy. "Honey, your job in the Army takes you all over the world. This is the first time in years you've been less than six hours from us, and we still haven't seen you in six months."

His cheeks burned from the shameful truth. She was right. He'd avoided coming home like the plague. "I'm sorry, I—"

"Jared, you don't have to apologize. You're almost twenty-seven years old. You've been on your own serving our country for nearly a decade. It's impossible to be more proud of you."

He returned to his seat on the edge of the bed. How could she be proud? If she really knew how messed up he was, she'd be downright ashamed, just like his father. "Mom, I—"

"I want you to be happy, Jared."

He shook his head. "It's not that easy." How could he make her understand without destroying what she thought of him?

"Sure it is. You should settle down. Start a family. Get a dog."

Jared laughed as he thought of the stray Michael had found. "Well, I have the dog, though I have no idea what to do with him until my papers come through."

His mother tilted her head to the side, and deep lines dug into her forehead. "You aren't re-enlisting?"

"No, ma'am. Eight years is enough. I'm ready to be a civilian again." He'd made up his mind a few months back, but everything with Michael had him rethinking the decision. "After this past week, I'm sure. It's time I move on to the next chapter of my life."

A quivering smile broke across her face, and her eyes puddled with tears, making his heart ache.

"Please don't cry, Mom." He leaned in and kissed her cheek.

"Do you have any idea how many sleepless nights I've had since you left for boot-camp? Two tours in that God-forsaken desert. I'd never been more proud than when I saw a news report, knowing you were saving lives, and never more thankful than when the phone rang and you were on the other end." She squeezed his cheeks together and kissed him.

"I'm sorry you worried so much."

She inhaled deep, her brow jutting upward with noticeable pride. "That's what mothers do."

"Well, I don't want you to worry anymore."

"That will never happen. Parents worry."

Jared wondered if that were true of his father as well. He nodded instead of voicing his doubt.

"Fall in love, son." She skimmed her hand over his. "Let yourself *be* loved."

A lump of air lodged in the back of his throat. He wanted so badly to share his life with her. He needed so badly to make her smile. "Mom, I – I don't know if that will ever be possible. I had a chance, but I really messed it up."

"Jared," she said with a sharp tone that he recognized right away. The "*I mean business*" tone she had used when he was a child, and even now, he sat up straight and listened.

"Yes, ma'am?"

"Whatever you did, fix it."

He shook his head. "It's not that easy."

"Son, if you don't tell him you love him, how will he ever know?"

What? Had he heard her right? Jared's entire body began to shake. "Ma'am?"

Tears streamed down her cheeks. "Nobody knows a man like his mother. The way you and Michael look at each other—" She huffed out an exhale. "Whew. It took my breath away."

He couldn't hold back the tears any longer. "I'm so sorry, Mom." He buried his face in the blankets covering her stomach and cried like he had as a child when his puppy died of Parvo.

Warm, loving fingers ran through his hair, and his mother shushed him as she always did when the pain became too much to bear. "There's nothing to be sorry for, Jared."

He lifted his chin and peered up at her through the blur of tears. "I know it's wrong, but I—"

"Son, love is never wrong."

Jared shook his head. "But, people will judge you for my choices."

Her brow creased again. "What people?"

"I don't know? Your friends. Family. The world."

Maureen laughed. "My friend's kids are far from perfect. And as far as family goes, well your aunt and I have been expecting this for years. It took you a while longer than it did us to see it."

"What?"

"Son, I'm your mother. I'm not dumb, and I'm not blind. I know my kid."

Jared rose from the bed and began to pace back and forth. *Am I dreaming?* The memory of his dad's face when he and Michael emerged from the backseat of the car, moments after making love, entered his mind. "But Dad—"

Maureen sat up straight. "Your father will come around. He's set in his ways, but he loves you."

She didn't know. She hadn't seen him. She hadn't heard what he said. "You don't understand."

"Your dad's old-fashioned, raised by a tyrant of a man who never settled for anything less than perfection. Why do you think he's always been so strict, but your uncle is so laid back?"

Jared hadn't a clue. He'd often wondered that himself growing up. Jared thought of the ice cream bin at the store by the lake-house and how easy-going and fun his uncle was and how angry it always made his dad. Polar opposites yet brought up in the same household.

"Your father was older and therefore a natural pleaser. Your uncle got to be the rebel. Your dad may seem unapproachable, but if you talk to him he'll eventually come around."

She had no idea how wrong she was. "He knows, Mom."

Her eyes widened. "What do you mean, he knows?"

"He saw me with Michael, when he first made it to the command tent. He saw us standing together, and trust me, he won't come around."

"What did he say?"

"He told me never to tell you because it would kill you."

Maureen laughed. "Jonathan Prophet and his flair for drama." She shook her head. "Don't worry about what he said. Be yourself, and love like there's no tomorrow, son. I would think after this tragedy you'd understand how important it is."

Jared eased over to her bedside as the door to the room opened. He held his breath as his father walked into the room.

"Dad?" He gave him a nod. "I'm glad to see you're okay."

"A very close call, but as long as your mother is alive and well, we've proved we can weather pretty much any storm."

"Is that so, Jon Prophet?" His mother's tone became cold and accusing.

Jared stood by her bed and held her hand. He lifted his chin, trying his best to appear strong and capable.

"That's right." Jonathan nodded.

"So if our son decided to share something important about his life with his mother, I wouldn't die, would I?"

An uneasy thread of angst spiraled up Jared's spine.

"Die?" His father cleared his throat, and his face reddened in the fluorescent lighting. "Why would you say that?" He glanced over at Jared like a deer caught in headlights.

"Dad," Jared said as he stepped toward him. "I'm sorry if I'm not the man you wanted me to be." A slow burn stung his eyes. "I never meant to dishonor our family."

His father's shoulders slumped, and his gaze lowered to the floor. "I don't know what you're talking about."

"Jon." Maureen raised her voice.

His father's expression hardened. "I'm not having this conversation with you here. Not with your mother in a hospital bed, our home demolished and our lives in such shambles. It's too much, Jared." He turned away. "Too much…"

Jared's heartbeat boomed to a near deafening level. "I understand." He leaned down and kissed his mom. "I'll call you when I get back to base."

"Don't leave it like this, Jared. Please?"

Jared smoothed his fingers through her golden curls. "It's okay. I love you." He turned away and charged through the door.

The long hallway became a blur, along with everything else Jared zoomed past as he made his way out to his car.

The dog sat up as soon as the keys rattled the lock.

Jared sat down behind the wheel and gripped it tight. His entire body shivered. Why had he let that go? His mother had practically laid out the red carpet for him to stand up for himself, and what did he do? He ran like the coward he'd been all his life.

Jared slammed his fist onto the steering wheel. "Fuck!" *Why didn't I say something? Anything?* Anger boiled within his gut. "You had your chance. God dammit!"

A wet nose nuzzled the back of his arm as the dog tried to offer comfort. He reached over and rubbed him behind the ears. "Thanks for the support, boy, but I don't think it's gonna help matters much."

Jared jumped at the startling sound of a knock on the driver's side window. He glanced over to see his father standing by the door.

Jared took a deep breath and exited the vehicle. He closed the door behind him and leaned against it.

"What I said before, when I saw you and your friend talking…" His father shook his head. "I…I can't say it's okay, and we'll work it out, Jared."

"I don't expect you to. I'm sorry I've been such a disappointment to you all these years, and then I make things worse by being… by being what I am."

Jonathan Prophet stepped closer and tilted his

head to the side. His chin quivered, and his shoulders slumped. "*What* you are?"

"Yes, Dad. What I am." Jared folded his arms across his chest. "I'm…" Jared swallowed hard. "I'm gay, Dad, and I won't ever be anything else."

"What do you mean you won't ever be anything else?"

"I won't ever be normal. I won't ever bring some girl home to introduce to you and mom, and I won't ever be a father like you… like real men are supposed to be." Jared struggled not to cry. Why add insult to injury?

"Jared, that isn't my main concern."

Jared lowered his arms to his side as a feeling of defeat and confusion sank in. "Then what is?"

"This is all my fault. If only I had protected you more when you were young then you wouldn't be struggling like this now."

"Are you serious? Dad, you kept the training wheels on my bike until I turned nine. Hell, you drove me to school and picked me up every day until I went to high school because you insisted the school bus was too dangerous."

"It *was* too dangerous." Jonathan said loudly, then looked around as though ashamed of his outburst.

"No, Dad. It was no more dangerous than any other form of transportation. The only difference was that you weren't in control."

"Look, I did my best to protect you. I insisted you wear your helmet when the training wheels came off your bike. I saw to it you had the best swimming lessons. I even followed the Driver's Ed car when you were getting your learner's permit to make sure the teacher had the proper experience to teach you. I—I…"

Jared's pulse raced. His dad had missed the point. For everything he did to protect Jared, his inattention to the things that really mattered had caused Jared the worst pain of his life. His dad hadn't protected him when it really counted, when Jared had needed his father the most.

It was more important Jared be well behaved. More important to be seen and not heard. More important for Jared to learn lessons the hard way, lessons that would build character and not waste time.

"Oh yeah? You protected me, huh?" His blood boiled and fury surged from somewhere so deep, Jared had never even known it was there. "Where were you when Mark Burns and his buddy took turns molesting me?" The words blurted before he could retract them. "You only had to toss a fucking ball around in the yard with your son, but you couldn't be bothered with such a waste of time. So Mark stepped up. Mark, the cool older boy, was more than happy to give the twelve year old neighbor kid attention, and he sure reminded me of all the possible ways to repay him for his friendship."

All color drained from Jonathan Prophet's face. "Mark Burns?" He placed his hand on the hood of the car as if to steady himself. "He was a kid."

"Yeah, sixteen." Jared plodded back and forth between his car and the truck parked beside his. "By the time he moved away, he and his friend had taught me things no kid should ever know."

"H-how long?"

"Over a year and a half." Jared punched the trunk of his car.

Jonathan brought a trembling hand to his mouth and looked as though he would be ill. "Is that why you're…?" The sentence trailed off.

"Why I'm gay?" Jared scoffed. "You would think so, and I did, up until a few days ago. But no, I'm pretty sure I would feel the way I do whether that had happened or not."

"Son, I'm…I'm sorry."

"Sorry?" Jared shrugged. "For what?"

"For failing you."

"You didn't fail me, Dad. You just didn't pay attention. But even if you had and even if the bad stuff never happened, I'd still be me, and I'd still be gay; and I'd still be your biggest disappointment."

Jonathan's expression turned to one of pain. "Disappointment? No, Jared you have never been a disappointment." He inched toward his son. "I only wanted to make sure you were a better man than me."

Jared listened, but he had no clue what his father meant. "I don't see how controlling my every move or flat out ignoring me is ever good for any kid."

"If I kept my distance, I'd never hit you."

What? "I don't understand."

His dad drew in a deep breath. "There always had to be examples in our house. My dad made sure we understood how important rules were, and as the oldest, I learned the lessons early on, for me and your uncle."

Jared's stomach swirled. "Grandpa hit you?"

"Your grandfather became a very different man after his stroke. Before then, our home resembled a war zone. You're uncle lucked out, too young to remember most of the bad years."

Jared had never heard this story. It explained so much, perhaps even his own violent streak. "Does Mom know?"

"Of course she does. It's probably why she makes so many damned excuses for my bad behavior."

Jared's heavy heart slowed as remorse settled inside. Maybe he'd been too hard on his dad all these years. "I'm sorry that happened to you."

Jonathan squeezed Jared's shoulder. "Jared, I may

not understand this thing with you, but I will always love you."

Jared's head swam with overwhelming emotions. In twenty-six years, his father had never said those words to him. "What?"

"I love you, and it may take some getting used to, but I want to find a way to understand. I want to find a way to be the father you need me to be."

Tears burned Jared's eyes. "That's how I've always felt. I wanted to be the son you needed *me* to be." *Is this really happening?*

Jonathan Prophet pulled his son close and hugged him hard.

Jared's knees weakened, and he thought he would collapse.

His dad held firm and tightened his grip. "I've got you, son." He kissed the top of Jared's head. "I'll always have you."

Raw, deep, painful emotions erupted within Jared's heart, and he held onto his father for dear life. "Dad," he sobbed. "I love you."

"I know you do, Jared." Jonathan pulled away, cupped Jared's cheeks in both of his hands and searched Jared's eyes. "We'll figure this out together. Your mother and I will do whatever you need to make this easier. I don't want to lose you."

"You won't lose me as long as I know I'm okay in your eyes."

"Son, you're perfect. You are the most amazing man I've ever had the pleasure of knowing, and I am in awe to know something so unbelievable came from me."

"What can I say?" Jared chuckled and rubbed his teary eyes. "I am my father's son."

Jonathan laughed. "Let's hope for your sake there's more of your mother in there than me."

Jared nodded and laughed. "She would probably agree."

A long silence passed between father and son until the dog's whimper snagged Jared's attention.

"What are you going to do with a dog on base?"

Jared took a deep breath to compose himself. "I need to find him a home. I'm expecting my retirement papers anytime and have no idea where I'll go once they come through."

"You're not re-enlisting?"

"No, sir. I'm moving on. Mom suggested I settle down and keep the dog, but…"

"Well, we have several days before your mother will be well enough to drive to Florida. I planned to hide out at the lake-house until then. Why don't we keep him for a few days?"

"Wow, okay." Jared reached through the open window and rubbed behind the dog's ear. "You know, I still have over a week left before I have to return from leave. If you're up to it, I'd sure like to do some fishing."

Jonathan's eyes widened, and he smiled. "I'd like that."

"Good." He hugged his dad. "I guess I'll head up there tonight. My friends and I left in a hurry because of the storm. Some broken tree limbs need cutting, so I'll take care of it for you."

"That sounds good." He patted Jared on the shoulder. "Thank you."

Jared leaned against the car and watched his father walk back toward the hospital. Only one thing remained on his mind now – figuring out how to fix what he'd messed up with Michael. He only had a few days to make it right.

Jared reached into his car and fumbled for his phone. He dialed the number and waited.

"Hello?" The voice on the other end answered.

"Alana?"

"Yeah?"

"This is Jared."

"Jared? Is everything okay?"

"That depends."

"On what?"

Jared sighed deeply. "I fucked up, and I really need your help."

"No shit."

TYLER ROBBINS

Chapter Fifteen

"Have you heard from him?"

Michael glared at Alana as she plopped down on the sofa next to him. "Seriously?"

She cocked one brow. "Gees, I just thought I'd ask."

"Alana, he sounded pretty clear about what he said." Michael shifted around and laid his head in her lap.

"I'm sorry." She gingerly ran her fingers through his hair.

Michael turned over and pressed his face into her stomach to hide his frown.

The rattling of keys sounded on the other side of the front door. Joel stopped and folded his arms across his chest, eyeing the two of them snuggled so close on the couch. "Should I be worried?"

Michael quickly moved his hand up to Alana's neck, pulled her down to him and kissed her on the lips. "Shit, guess the cat's out of the bag, now."

Joel sarcastically chortled as he approached. "You wouldn't know what to do with that kind of cat if it jumped out and bit you."

Michael jumped to his feet. "Well my luck with men hasn't gotten me very far. Maybe I should mix things up a little."

Joel walked around behind the sofa and kissed Alana's neck. "If I thought for one second you were serious, I'd beat your ass for messing around with my girl."

Michael's cheeks heated. "She's definitely worth an ass beating."

"Damn straight," Alana said as she got to her feet as well. "Not to change the subject, but since they finally drained the pool and cleaned up the debris from the storm, I'm ready to relax. I also recall being promised significant sun-bathing time for hooking us up with my parents' condo while they're in Hawaii."

"The lovely lady has a point. We did promise, and if she still has that white bikini, maybe I should test out my hetero-meter."

"You're hetero-what?" Joel crinkled his nose.

"It's a meter we use to measure how gay we are." He stuck his hand down his pants to provide a visual aid. "If the flag goes up…" He extended his thumb against the front of his shorts. "Then we're not as gay as we think."

Alana snickered. "Now that's hot."

Joel's mouth gaped open. "Are you fucking with me?"

Michael winked. "What do you think?"

"I think I'm not leaving you and Alana alone anymore. You may trip, fall and accidentally discover you're a cat person after all."

Alana giggled.

"Here, kitty, kitty." Michael beckoned her to him with a curled index finger.

Alana responded with a playful purr, sidled up to him and nuzzled under his chin.

Joel's eyes widened, and his head shook like a dash-mounted bobble toy. "You both better stop."

Laughter filled the room as Michael returned to the sofa and stretched out.

Alana disappeared into the bedroom.

Michael grabbed a tennis ball lying on the coffee table and tossed it up in the air. "Joel, seriously, if she wears that white bikini, we're both going to the pool to keep an eye on her."

"I know that's right." Joel gave Michael a high five and sat in the chair across from the sofa. "So have you heard anything?"

"You, too?" Michael dropped the ball, slammed a throw pillow over his face and screamed into it.

"Sorry, man. You're my best friend. I only want to know if you're ever gonna get what you want."

Michael removed the pillow. "Not everybody gets everything they want,"

"Well, you should, and I don't want to add insult to injury, but I talked to Raul today."

This piece of information caught Michael's attention. He sat up and leaned toward Joel. "And? Did Jared show up back at base yet?"

"No," Joel shook his head. "But Jared's name did come across his desk in an admin file."

Michael shrugged. "So, what does that mean?"

"It means Jared's done. His retirement came through. With this leave still active and thirty days accrued, he's technically already out."

Seriously? "What?" Michael sat back and stared at the ceiling. "He never said a word."

"Sorry, man."

How could Jared have started this thing if he knew he wouldn't be around? "I wonder what else he neglected to tell me?"

"Who knows, maybe he would have told you at the lake-house if all hell hadn't broken loose with the storm."

Michael gave Joel a skeptical glare. "Yeah, that would have been great pillow talk. *'So glad you fell for me. Oh, by the way, I'm retiring, so don't get too attached.'*"

"Dude, that's harsh."

"No shit." Michael jumped to his feet, his blood pumping. "Fuck, I need to run."

"When Alana comes out, you can take your

frustration out on a few serious laps in the pool."

"*Alana* won't be getting in the pool." Alana emerged from the bedroom with her arms folded across her chest.

Michael turned around. "Why?"

"Because I can't find the bag that had my swim suits, I.D. and wallet."

"What do you mean? Is it in the car?" Joel went over to her.

"No, we unloaded everything from the car when we got here. We haven't been able to swim, and I haven't needed my wallet until now."

"Where do you think it is?" Joel asked.

"My guess is the lake-house."

"Jared's lake-house?" Michael's stomach flip-flopped.

"That's the last place I saw it."

"Can't you buy another bikini?"

"Not without money, Mikey. Besides, my wallet had my bank I.D., too. If that fell into the wrong hands…"

"Ooh, that might spell disaster for the banking system as we know it." Joel's eyes widened as he teased her.

Alana playfully punched his arm. "No, but it would spell disaster for my job."

"Damn. What are you going to do?" Michael asked.

Her nose crinkled. "Would you call him?"

Michael's heart skipped a beat. "I'm not callin' him. You call him."

"Seriously, Mikey. How old are you?"

"Old enough to know not to kick a dead horse."

"Eww! Gross."

"Alana, Michael can't call Jared. It would break

rule number sixteen of the bro-code."

"Bro-code?" Alana asked with both fists planted firmly on her hips.

"Yes, rule sixteen dash B states that a man can never initiate contact with the girl… er…" He nervously glanced over at Michael before correcting himself, "Significant other who intentionally and with great malice breaks his heart because they want to be a bitch – I mean, ass."

Alana pursed her lips and narrowed her gaze. "Is that so?" She eyed them both.

Michael responded with an enthusiastic nod. "It's in the Bro-code handbook."

"Well…" She strolled over to the chair and sat down. "I would never want to cause a cataclysmic event capable of offsetting the evolutionary process of two exceedingly advanced imbeciles, so I'll make the call myself."

"Was there an insult in there, because it sort of felt like there may have been a negative vibe mixed in with all those big words?" Joel asked as he bent over and kissed her cheek.

"Cell phone?" She rolled her eyes and presented an overturned hand as though expecting manna from heaven.

Joel handed her his cell phone, and she got up and headed to the bedroom.

Michael and Joel both followed.

As she reached the door, she quickly spun around. "Oh, no, you aren't listening to my conversation. If you wanted to know what Jared has to say, you should have called him yourself." She pushed against Michael's chest to move him back, shut the door behind her and locked it.

"Damn. Maybe I should have called." Michael chewed the inside of his cheek as the muscles tightened in his neck.

"No way, man. In this case, you're better off making him suffer."

"Yeah, but that's just it. I'm the one suffering, not him." He plopped back onto the couch and resumed his former position. "I'd bet he's not suffering at all."

****

"Tell me why I had to come with you again?" Michael asked from the backseat of Alana's Dodge Charger.

"Because Jared said the key to the house is hidden in some fort out in the woods, and you're the only one who knows where that is."

Michael sat back with his stomach twisting into a million tiny knots as the lake-house came into view. "Seriously, it's not that hard to find."

"For fuck's sake, Michael, will you grow a pair already? Go get the key so we can get Alana's bag, and then we're outta here."

Michael huffed a heavy sigh. "Okay, okay."

The car came to a stop, and he cautiously looked around for signs of Jared.

The house stood solemn, and there didn't seem to be anyone around. *So far, so good.* The fallen tree limbs had been cleared, and there appeared to be fresh ashes at the fire site down by the water's edge. "Looks like somebody cleaned up the mess from the storm."

"Looks that way," Alana said as she exited the car.

Michael stepped out behind her. "He's not supposed to be here, right?"

"He said he's helping his parents with their move to Florida."

"Florida? I wonder if that's where he's planning to move now that he's a civilian?" .More unanswered questions entered his mind. How much longer would Jared's life-decisions be an issue?

"Who knows? I didn't ask." Alana leaned against the hood of her car.

Joel joined her, and they immediately started kissing.

"Are y'all coming with me?"

"Hell no, bro. We've been cooped up in the car for hours. I plan to stay right here and make out with my girl."

Michael dipped his head, disappointed. "Thanks for the support."

"Anytime," Joel said as he and Alana resumed kissing.

Michael kicked at a pinecone as he hiked toward the woods. He shoved his hands into his front pockets and kept his head down. Memories, good and bad, quickly rose to the forefront of his mind. He never really thought he'd ever be back there again, and being there without Jared felt strange.

He looked for the criss-crossed trees and made his way toward them. The woods looked different somehow. Not quite as mysterious or lonely as it once had when Jared first brought him there. Of course, the first time had been in the dark and the next, in the middle of a serious storm. The world looked a lot different in the light.

He slowed his pace as the remains of the fort came into view. A fresh layer of dry pine straw dusted the top of the twisted pile. Michael stood before the heap and thought of the promise he'd made Jared. Then promise to rebuild it. *Guess that won't happen now.*

"Hey," an all too familiar voice spoke behind him.

Michael spun around to find Jared Prophet standing before him, in the flesh. "What are you doing here?"

"Waiting for you."

Michael's insides turned to a quivering mush. "Why?" Did he want to threaten him some more? Yell at him? Tell him to disappear?

"I wanted to tell you something."

Michael's chest tightened. "I think you've said all there is to say." He forced his legs to move and started back toward the house.

"Will you wait?" Jared raised his voice triggering a ripple effect of emotions to whirl within Michael's body.

He stopped, but didn't turn to face Jared. His ears rang as though his head would explode from the unbearable shock of coming face to face with Jared after all that had happened.

"I fucked up, man."

"No shit." Michael closed his eyes and shook his head. *Unbelievable.*

"Will you look at me?" Jared's voice cracked.

Michael took a deep breath and slowly turned around. "What do you want from me, Jared?"

He stepped closer causing Michael's heart to boom. Michael balled his fists at his sides, half expecting a fight and half expecting to crumble into a pathetic mess.

"I want you." Jared's gaze concentrated on the ground between them.

"What?" Had he heard him right? "Is this some twisted joke?"

"No." Jared shook his head. "I want you." He inched closer.

"Jared, I swear if you're playing some sort of sadistic game to fuck with my head I'll—"

In an instant, Jared's mouth assailed Michael's, and his tongue plunged in deep.

Michael's knees buckled, and he staggered back;

but Jared caught him and pulled him closer.

"I love you, Michael. I love you like I've never loved another person my entire life."

Michael fought back tears as Jared's words bounced around in his mind. Going against everything his body wanted, Michael pushed away. "I can't hide." He squared his shoulders. "I *won't* hide." His jaw clenched tight.

"I'm not asking you to."

Jared reached for him, but Michael pulled away. "Why? Because your parents are moving to Florida and you've retired from the Army?" He stepped eased back. "Is it easier to pretend you're straight if I'm off in some other country and the rest of the world doesn't have to see us together?"

"No. My parents know all about you," Jared whispered.

Michael's stomach fluttered. *Is he telling the truth?* "Your dad—?"

Jared nodded. "He knows it all. He knows about what happened to me, and he knows how I feel about you."

"And he's fine with that?"

"Not entirely. He needs time, but he promised to try." Jared's chin quivered. "He and I had a really serious talk before they left for Florida. In fact…" He looked at Michael with one eyebrow cocked. "The next time you have a few days, they want me to take you to Florida to officially meet them. I told them we'd try to make it before Christmas."

"Christmas?" Michael's mouth watered with anticipation. Christmas was still a few months away. What did this mean? Dizziness engulfed his senses.

"I love you, Michael, and I want to be with you. Possibilities Michael hadn't had time to contemplate bombarded his mind. How would this work? "I still have two years on my contract."

"So?"

"So, you're a civilian. How would we ever see each other?"

"Alana's a civilian, and she and Joel see each other all the time."

"But she has an apartment near the base."

Jared dug in his pocket and brought out a set of keys. "So do I."

Michael's heart beat double time. "Where?"

"Six apartments down from Alana."

"How?"

"She hooked me up two days ago."

Fire burned the back of Michael's throat. "Seriously?"

"Wherever you go, I go." Jared reached for Michael's arm and drew him to him. "What are you thinking?" His brow furrowed, and he skimmed his finger over Michael's lips, searching his eyes.

"I'm wondering of this is a dream."

Jared kissed him again, and Michael instinctively pushed him to the ground. His cock pulsed, and his need to have Jared completely engulfed his every thought. "I love you."

Jared's chest heaved as his breathing escalated. "I'm so sorry I put you through hell." He ran his hand down the front of Michael's jeans and unzipped his zipper.

Chills ricocheted across Michael's flesh. "Shh." He pressed his thumb into Jared's mouth. "Don't talk."

Jared wrapped his tongue around Michael's thumb and sucked it while freeing Michael's throbbing cock.

Michael gasped as Jared released his thumb,

lowered his head and encircled the head of his dick with his hot lips. Michael thrust his hips upward, jamming himself deeper within Jared's mouth. His ass cheeks tightened as a tingling surge rushed up the length of his prick, and pre-cum seeped from the tip.

Jared licked it clean, moved to Michael's balls and jumbled them in his mouth, making them dance on his tongue.

Michael moaned. "Let me inside you."

Jared stopped, crawled to his knees and slowly unfastened his pants, allowing them to drop to the ground. His hardened cock bobbled up and down, and Jared lifted his shirt, exposing those rock-hard abs Michael savored so much. He ran his hands down his stomach and glared down at Michael through hooded eyes. Taking his cock in his hand, Jared stroked it for Michael. "Everything I have is yours, kid." A cocky smile spread across his face.

Michael rose to his knees and pressed his cock against Jared's. "I got your kid right here." He finally told Jared what he'd wanted to tell him for days, then kissed him.

Sticks and leaves rustled beneath them. "Stand up," Michael said.

Jared did as he was told without argument or question, which only made Michael's balls burn with desire.

Michael stood as well, then turned Jared around.

Jared leaned over and propped against a tree, which only drew Michael's attention to his ass. Deep indentions formed in the sides of Jared's firm, perfectly shaped ass. Michael squatted and kissed both cheeks then spread them apart. He ran his tongue up and down the crack, paying close attention to the tightened hole. Probing the area, Michael moved back and forth from delving deep into the hole and flicking his tongue over Jared's gooseflesh riddled skin. "Tell me you love me," Michael whispered.

Jared panted. "I love you."

Usually the more submissive of the two, Michael's hand shook as an air of dominance overtook his mind. "Tell me you want me."

"God, I want you so bad." Desperation echoed in Jared's tone.

Michael spat on his fingers and gently inserted the tip of his middle finger into Jared's ass while kissing and licking the area.

"Fuck, baby." Jared's breathing became labored. "Please don't tease me."

Michael pushed inside, aiming for Jared's sweet spot. The instant he nicked it, Jared shrieked. "Yes. There." He sucked air in through his teeth.

Michael flicked it again, and Jared's body shuddered. "Please?"

Michael rose and cupped his balls, allowing his cock to dangle against Jared's ass. He then gripped the base and nudged it toward the middle of Jared's crack. Jared deserved a little teasing after all he'd put Michael through.

"Tell me what you want."

Jared glanced over his shoulder. "I want you. Only you."

Michael was about to end Jared's suffering when Jared reached back, grabbed Michael's cock and drew it into him, then pushed himself back onto it, engulfing Michael with his ass.

Michael's vision blurred as his dick disappeared all the way to the base within Jared's hot, tight ass. He gasped. "Shit, Jared."

Jared rocked back and forth on Michael's cock. "I

told you not to tease me."

Michael gripped his hips and jammed himself in deeper.

Jared moaned. "Again."

Michael shoved in deeper, grunting loud with every thrust.

Both men groaned and writhed as the motion quickened.

Michael's balls slapped against the back if Jared's thighs, and his heart pounded and sweat dripped from his brow as he pumped feverishly. He leaned his head back as the pressure grew.

"I'm coming." He panted as a burst of heat erupted from his cock, filling Jared's ass with his seed.

Jared stilled and after taking in a few deep breaths he eased himself off Michael's cock and faced him. "Finish me, baby."

Michael glanced down at Jared's engorged prick in his hand, the tip glistening with his clear, sweet essence. He lowered himself to his knees and began to suck him off.

Jared caressed the back of Michael's head. "I love you so fucking much it hurts."

The words echoed in Michael's ears, encouraging him to lick, suck and please Jared to the best of his ability. By the time Jared came, Michael had been so engrossed in making sure he'd fulfilled his lover's desires, he hadn't even realized he'd swallowed every drop Jared's satisfied cock had to offer.

Both men, collapsed onto the ground, and Jared cradled Michael in his arms.

Michael looked up. "This is nothing like how I expected my day to go."

"Funny." Jared laughed. "It's exactly how I planned it."

"We can make this work, right?"

"Michael, I will move heaven and earth to make you happy."

"So what now?"

Jared exhaled hard. "Well, since Joel and Alana left you here, we can either finish out your leave here, or go back to base and move me into my new apartment."

Michael shook his head. "Joel and Alana left?"

"They left the second you disappeared into the woods. We're totally alone."

"Of course." Michael grinned. Naturally, Alana and Joel already knew about the reconciliation. Hell, they probably helped plan it.

Michael pondered his decision. "I say we stay and take advantage of some alone time."

"Good idea."

Jared got to his feet and reached down for Michael's hand.

Michael glared at it then looked up at him. "You do realize I'm not a girl, right?"

Jared laughed. "Trust me, with the way my ass ached the other day, I definitely know you're not a girl."

"Now you know how I felt." Michael accepted his hand and jumped to his feet.

Jared jerked him close. "I've always known how you felt…but I had to show you how I felt."

Michael kissed him. "You have, Jared." He smiled at Jared as they both redressed.

"Let's go inside. I'm about to starve to death."

Michael took Jared's hand and followed him out of the woods.

A strange, but familiar sound reverberated through the trees. "Jared?"

"Huh?" He looked back over his shoulder.

"Do you hear a dog barking?"

"That would be the Marlboro Man."

"The what?" A movement down by the lake captured Michael's attention. "I don't believe it."

The stray dog he'd rescued earlier in the week stood on the pier barking at the water.

As they approached, he spotted them and came running.

Michael dropped to his knees and greeted the fluffy white dog with friendly scratches behind his ears. "He looks so different."

"Yeah, it took my dad and me three hours to clean him up before my mom would allow him in the house."

"Wow." Michael never expected Jared to keep him. Hell, he didn't think Jared even liked the mutt. "Marlboro Man is so much more fitting than Sir Muttly."

"I named him that in honor of the night I fell in love with you in the bathroom of the rec center."

Michael stood again and smiled. "Oh, that was the night, huh?"

"Don't act like you didn't know."

"Oh, I knew all right, but I didn't know if you did."

Jared caressed Michael's cheek. "It took a little work, but I got there."

Michael leaned into his hand. "I'm so glad you did."
****

Jared stood on the pier as Michael played catch with Marlboro Man up by the house. He gazed out at the water and allowed his mind to take in the glorious sunset as shimmering orange and golden hues danced across every ripple of the water.

"Yeah." Jared sighed and bit his bottom lip. He'd finally figure it out.

In this moment, when his mind finally accepted

what his heart had always known, Jared knew without a doubt…it had all been worth it.

Pain and despair no longer had a place in his life, and though he had no idea what tomorrow held, for the first time in his life, he didn't worry if he'd be able to handle it, if he'd be the man he needed to be to see it through.

Jared was an honorable man.

Michael had taught him that much, and as long as Michael always saw him that way, all things were possible. No matter how corny it sounded, they could have it all, and it was a wonderful feeling to finally believe it.

The End

~A personal note from the author~

Honor is defined as an abstract concept entailing a perceived quality of worthiness and respectability that affects both the social standing and the self-evaluation of an individual or group such as a family, school, regiment or nation.

Accordingly, individuals are assigned worth and stature based on the harmony of their actions with a specific code of honor, and the moral code of the society at large.

Honor is adherence to what is right.

While writing this story, Jared and Michael took this author on an emotional journey like nothing I had ever experienced, and I found myself constantly reflecting on the lives of the men and women who serve in our nation's military.

It has always been my belief that race, religion or sexual orientation of an individual, hold no bearing on their ability to do their job efficiently and with honor.

It's been a long time coming, and though our Nation still has a long road ahead, the repeal of the military's policy of *"Don't ask, Don't tell"* was a giant step in the direction of equality for all.

This story is dedicated to all of those service members who were and still are personally affected by this policy because of who they've chosen to love.

I hear you; I support you; and I am humbled by all that you do to protect our nation. Thank you.

The End

www.tylerrobbins.org

TYLER ROBBINS

Evernight Publishing

www.evernightpublishing.com